S0-BYV-120

SHREK

by Ellen Weiss

DREAMWORKS.

PUFFIN BOOKS

Published by the Penguin Group

Penguin Putnam Books for Young Readers,

345 Hudson Street, New York, New York 10014, U.S.A.

Penguin Books Ltd, 27 Wrights Lane, London W8 5TZ, England

Penguin Books Australia Ltd, Ringwood, Victoria, Australia

Penguin Books Canada Ltd, 10 Alcorn Avenue, Toronto, Ontario, Canada M4V 3B2

Penguin Books (N.Z.) Ltd, 182-190 Wairau Road, Auckland 10, New Zealand

Penguin Books Ltd, Registered Offices: Harmondsworth, Middlesex, England

Published by Puffin Books,

a division of Penguin Putnam Books for Young Readers, 2001

1 3 5 7 9 10 8 6 4 2

TM & © 2001 DreamWorks

Text by Ellen Weiss

Illustrations by Lawrence Hamashima

All rights reserved

Puffin Books ISBN 0-14-131249-1

Printed in the United States of America

Except in the United States of America, this book is sold subject to
the condition that it shall not, by way of trade or otherwise, be lent, re-sold,
hired out, or otherwise circulated without the publisher's prior consent in any form
of binding or cover other than that in which it is published and without a similar
condition including this condition being imposed on the subsequent purchaser.

one
Cash for Creatures

nce upon a time, there was a lovely princess.

But she had an enchantment upon her of a fearful sort, which could only be broken by love's first kiss. She was locked away in a castle guarded by a terrible, firebreathing dragon.

Many brave knights had attempted to free her from this dreadful prison, but none had prevailed. She waited in the Dragon's Keep, in the highest room of the tallest tower, for her true love—and true love's first kiss.

Sitting in his outhouse, Shrek regarded the storybook. It was a bit worn but still beautiful, bound in the finest leather. The page before him showed a picture of a lovely princess, holding up her billowing skirts and running through a field of flowers. In the background was a fairy-tale castle.

"Yeah—like that's ever gonna happen!" he chuckled to himself as he tore the page from the old book with his huge green hand. Well, he was out of paper in there anyhow—this page would do just fine.

As he emerged from the outhouse, Shrek yanked at a wedgie in his underwear. He was not a handsome fellow. But then, of course, he was an ogre, so this was to be expected. He was about seven feet tall, and solidly built. His skin was the color of week-old pea soup, his ears were strange trumpetlike things on stalks, and his teeth looked as if they could crush large rock. Probably because they could.

Being an ogre, Shrek was perfectly content with his looks. What did he care if the townspeople thought he was a horrid, fearsome monster? As long as they left him alone, he was happy.

As he walked back to his house, Shrek noticed that a page of the storybook was still stuck to his foot. Readjusting his underwear, he shook it off.

He paused for a moment to admire his humble abode. Though to the untrained eye it might have looked like a great, crooked heap of mud and sticks, it was in fact a perfect house for an ogre. He was proud of this house. He liked living in it, all by himself. This was why his home was surrounded by large, emphatic KEEP OUT signs.

Grabbing a huge bucket, Shrek set out to complete his morning routine. First came the mud shower. Using the bucket, he scooped up a hearty amount of rich mud from a giant mud puddle behind his hut and vigorously rubbed himself down with it.

When that was done, he focused on his teeth. Grabbing a bug from his toiletry jar, he squeezed it onto a bone and scrubbed away. Mmmm—bugpaste. He checked his smile, cracking the mirror loudly in the process. How perfect could life get?

Last, but not least, Shrek jumped into the mucky swamp pond. He lay back contentedly, and pretty soon the water around his rear end filled with absolutely horrible-smelling bubbles. As they rose up and burst around him, a relieved smile spread over Shrek's face. A second later, a few dead fish floated belly-up next to him. Shrek happily gathered them up. Could fishing get any easier?

When he climbed out of the pond, Shrek's huge green legs were covered in leeches. He pulled one off and tasted it. Yum.

Spotting a hollow log that floated in the pond, he snatched it up and used his gigantic hand to push the muddy gook from inside. A great pile of glop fell from the end. And inside the glop was—Yay! A mud squid, his favorite.

🪰

Sunset. The end of a perfect day. Shrek was busy with a painting project. Humming to himself, he delicately applied brush strokes to his creation, standing back every now and then to admire his work. When he was finished, he took the painting from the easel and hammered a stick to the back.

It was not a beautiful landscape, though. It was a sign. BEWARE, it warned. The letters were nice and big, so that any nincompoop could read them. This should do the trick. Nobody would dare intrude on his beloved privacy.

🪰

Meanwhile, in a quiet town not far from the swamp, things were not so peaceful. At that very moment, an angry mob was pouring out of the village pub. Tacked to the door of the pub was a sign that said, WANTED! CREATURES FOR CASH! On the poster was an image of an ogre.

Someone used a stick to draw a plan of attack onto the ground. Torches were lit. Pitchforks were raised, and when everybody was good and worked up, the mob of villagers headed into the forest—straight toward Shrek's swamp.

🪰

Shrek was blissfully ignorant of all this activity. As

the crowd tramped through the woods, the ogre ate his soup, lit his fire, and sat down beside it. As they neared his house, heedlessly trampling his KEEP OUT signs, he was biting off some nice fish heads.

Finally hearing a noise, Shrek looked out his window into the night. Shrek rolled his eyes and closed the curtain. What now?

The mob made its way quietly through the bushes, and then stopped. Warily, they parted the reeds in front of them to peer at Shrek's house.

One of them stepped forward determinedly. "All right," he whispered. "Let's get it!"

Alarmed, another villager grabbed his arm to stop him. "Whoa! Hang on!" he said. "Do you have any idea what that thing will do to you?"

"Yeah," a third villager piped up. "It'll grind your bones for its bread." The other villagers stared at him, momentarily unable to speak.

Then a voice broke the silence. "Actually," it said brightly, "that would be a giant."

Hearing this new voice, the villagers spun around. There was Shrek, standing nonchalantly behind them. The flickering light of the torch made him look *really* scary.

"Now, your ogres," he said in a friendly way, "they're much worse." He began advancing toward them now as he spoke, and his tone became more intense and terrifying as he got closer. "They'll make a suit from your freshly peeled skin," he continued. "They'll shave your liver, squeeze the jelly from your eyes. Actually, it's quite good on toast." The villagers began to back away, not quite as brave as they had been.

Finally one villager, summoning all his courage, leaped bravely forward, waving the torch in front of him. "Back! Back, beast! Back! I warn you," he shouted.

Shrek casually leaned away to avoid the torch, and watched the man with mild indifference. Eventually, tired of waving, the man held the torch threateningly in front of him. Shrek stuck out his tongue to moisten his thumb and forefinger and, reaching forward, gently snuffed out the torch.

As the villagers stood stunned, Shrek took advantage of the quiet to issue a tremendous, terrifying roar.

The villagers screwed their eyes closed and screamed for all they were worth. They screamed for so long, in fact, that Shrek was amused to notice that they were still screaming well after he had stopped roaring. Finally, when they'd petered out, he leaned down and whispered to them in a confidential way.

"Boo," he said.

Without missing a beat, they all turned and ran away, as fast as they could. Shrek watched them go, chuckling to himself. Then he sighed and headed back toward his house. When would they ever learn?

Before he reached his door, he noticed a small

poster that one of the villagers had dropped. He picked it up and read it.

It was a wanted poster. "Offering cash for creatures," it said.

Shrek wadded it up, tossed it aside, and headed back into his house. Shaking his head, he thought again—when would they ever learn?

two
Donkey on the Loose

ut the offer of cash for creatures was an attractive one, too attractive for the townspeople to ignore. Other denizens of this fairy-tale kingdom were easier to round up than ogres. That very day, the villagers began lining up at the trading post to collect their money. The place was bedlam.

A table had been set up in a clearing at the edge of the forest, and a captain was sitting behind it, doling out coins in exchange for the captured creatures.

A farmer, clutching a wanted poster of a dwarf, had brought a gaggle of fairy-tale dwarves with him. The captain tossed him several gold coins, and then jotted down the trade in his ledger book. "Next," he said. "Take them away." The dwarves were led off in shackles.

"Move it along," a guard prodded them as they shuffled away. "Come on."

"He ho, hi he," they sang mournfully, "dwarf prisoners are we. . . . He ho, hi he, dwarf prisoners are we. . . . "

A second farmer stepped up to the captain's table, shoving before him a witch tied with rope. Quickly, one of the guards grabbed her broom. "Give me that! Your flying days are over," he barked, snapping it in two over his knee.

The captain looked the witch over without much interest. "Twenty pieces of silver for the witch," he said. "Next."

The witch was immediately taken away, as the farmer collected his reward. "Lousy twenty pieces!" he grumbled to himself as he left. He hardly noticed the long line of people who still waited to sell their fairy-tale captives. There were two villagers with elves, an old man with a wooden puppet of a boy, an old woman with a donkey she called Donkey, a boy with a glowing fairy in a cage, and a burly peasant with three little pigs under his arms.

Beside the old woman, the donkey looked around nervously. He watched the witch being carted off in a wagon with the seven dwarves. Then, hearing a cry, he turned to see three bears. They were all in cages.

The baby bear reached for his mother as their cages were dragged apart. "This cage is too small!" he sobbed.

This was too much for Donkey. He turned beseechingly to the old woman who held his rope. "Please, don't turn me in!" he begged. "I'll never be stubborn again. I can change, please gimme another chance!"

"Ah, shut up, Donkey!" responded the old woman.

"Next!" said the captain.

The old man with the puppet stepped forward and plopped it down on the table.

"What have you got?" the captain asked.

"This little wooden puppet," the old man said.

"I'm not a puppet! I'm a real boy!" protested Pinocchio. Immediately, however, he began vibrating, and then, suddenly, his nose grew to five times its previous length.

"Five shillings for the possessed toy," offered the captain. "Take it away!"

"Father, please don't let them do this!" Pinocchio begged the old man. "Help me!" But it was too late. The old man was already counting his money.

"Next!" shouted the captain.

The old woman dragged the resisting donkey up to the table.

"What have you got?" said the captain.

"Well, I've got a talking donkey."

This actually got the captain to glance up from his ledger. He looked Donkey up and down. "Right," he said. "That'll be ten shillings if you can prove it."

Donkey swallowed hard and looked at the old woman, who was beginning to untie his rope.

"Go ahead, li'l fella," she urged.

Hesitating, Donkey looked at the old woman, and then to the captain. The captain looked back at Donkey and lifted an eyebrow.

"Well?" he said.

Donkey looked back at the captain. Saying nothing seemed to be his best option.

The old woman was beginning to sweat. "He's just a little nervous," she said nervously. "He's really quite a chatterbox." She bent down and slapped Donkey. "Talk, you boneheaded dolt! Talk!" she ordered him under her breath.

"That's it," said the captain impatiently. "I've heard enough. Guards!"

"He talks! He does!" cried the old woman. In desperation, she grabbed Donkey's lips and squeezed them. "I can talk. I love to talk!" she said, trying, like a bad ventriloquist, to make Donkey's mouth move. "I'm the talkiest darn thing you ever saw!"

The captain had heard enough. He motioned to his guards. "Get her out of my sight," he said.

The guards advanced on the old woman and dragged her off, screaming. "No!" she shrieked. "No! I swear. Let me go. He can talk! No! Wait!"

As she struggled, the old woman accidentally kicked the caged fairy from the hand of the boy who was waiting next on line. The cage went flying through the air and landed on Donkey's head, exploding fairy dust all over him.

He blinked, shocked at first, but then he began to smile. Something was happening to him, something amazing, something . . .

"Hey! I can fly!"

All heads turned to Donkey as he fluttered into the air above the crowd.

"He can fly!" cried Peter Pan.

"He can fly!" cried the three little pigs.

"He can talk!" noted the captain.

Smiling madly, Donkey began rising upward, swimming in the air like a dog treading water. "That's right, fool!" he called down from his vantage point safe above the crowd. "Now I'm a flying talking donkey. You might have seen a house fly, maybe even a super fly, but I bet you've never seen a *donkey* fly. Ha, ha!"

But actually, Donkey wasn't flying quite so well anymore, because the fairy dust was wearing off. Looking down, Donkey suddenly realized his predicament.

"Uh-oh," he said, falling hard right in front of the captain.

"Seize him!" ordered the captain.

The guards dove for Donkey, but he was already running for all he was worth into the woods. "After him! He's getting away!" They gave chase, led by the captain.

Donkey hurtled through the woods as fast as his legs could carry him, trees whizzing by on all sides. He looked over his shoulder. The soldiers were gaining. Donkey picked up speed. But before he could increase his lead . . . *wham!*

Donkey barreled straight into Shrek's butt. It was like hitting a wall. Donkey fell back onto his own rear end, the wind firmly knocked out of him.

three
You Gotta Have Friends

hrek had been hanging a new BEWARE sign on a tree at the edge of the forest. He wanted to be sure that no more mobs would be invading his swamp. He was just about done when Donkey ran into him.

Shrek looked down at Donkey. Donkey looked up at him, not quite sure what to make of the ogre.

Then the guards rounded the corner, screeching to a halt at the sight of Shrek. Donkey lost no time in darting behind the ogre. He'd already decided he'd much rather take his chances with the big green guy than with the guards.

"You there," said the captain, just a bit nervously. "Ogre."

"Yeah?" Shrek responded.

"By the order of Lord Farquaad," said the captain, looking more and more uncomfortable, "I am authorized to place you both under arrest and transport you to a designated resettlement facility."

Shrek looked down at him. "Oh, really? You and what army?"

The captain looked behind him, only to find that his men had deserted him. A terrified look spread across his face. Shrek just smiled. The captain gasped and turned in retreat.

As the captain ran off into the forest, Shrek shrugged and headed back toward his home, taking not the slightest notice of Donkey. But Donkey was no fool either. He smiled at his new hero and decided to follow.

Shrek continued on his way, unaware of the fact that the little donkey was following at a distance behind him. Finally Donkey summoned up his nerve and spoke.

"Can I say something to you?" he said. "Listen, you were really, really something back there! Incredible!"

Shrek stopped and turned, a little annoyed. "Are you talking to me?" he said.

But Donkey was now gone.

Good, Shrek thought. He didn't need an annoying talking donkey hanging around.

Shrek turned to continue on his way. And there was Donkey, right in front of him, beaming.

Donkey talked fast. "Yes! I was talkin' to you. Can I just tell you, you were really great back there, man, those guards, they thought they were all that! Then you showed up and . . . *bam*! They were tripping over themselves, crying like babes in the woods. It really made me feel good to see that."

"That's great," said Shrek with complete disinterest. "Really."

Donkey was really warming up now. "Man, it's good to be free," he said, stretching a little.

Shrek looked straight at him. "Why don't you go celebrate your freedom with your own friends?" he said. It was not a suggestion.

"But, uh . . . I don't have any friends. And I am not going out there by myself. Hey, wait a minute. I got a great idea. I'll stick with you. You're a mean, green fighting machine. Together we'll scare the spit out of anybody who crosses us!"

Shrek was finally fed up. He stopped and heaved a deep sigh. Why did he have to keep doing the ogre thing? Then he turned on Donkey and roared, waving his arms, doing the ogre act that he generally did to scare off unwanted visitors.

But Donkey was different from the others. Somehow, Donkey seemed to have decided that Shrek was his hero. And of course, as his hero, couldn't possibly mean that scary stuff. He must be just fooling around.

"Oh, wow!" Donkey said, still talking as fast as possible. "That was really scary. And, if you don't mind me saying, if that doesn't work, your breath certainly will get the job done. 'Cause you definitely need some Tic-tacs or something, 'cause your breath stinks! Man! You almost burned the hair off my nose. Just like the time—"

Shrek grabbed Donkey's muzzle and held it shut. But that didn't stop Donkey.

"—mime mi benb binbo be moods manm mi mied bo mgo," he continued as best he could.

Shrek was at a loss. This had never happened to him before. He let go and tried to walk away. But Donkey just kept talking, following along behind him.

"—and then I ate some rotten berries," he was yammering. "Man, I had some strong gases eking out of my butt that day. . ."

Shrek could not take it for one more second. He spun around to face Donkey. "Why are you following me?" he demanded.

"I'll tell you why." And with that, as Shrek looked on, speechless with horror, Donkey burst into song: *You gotta have friends—*

Donkey was really gathering steam now, but

Shrek cut him off. "*Stop singing!*" he yelled.

Donkey closed his mouth in shock.

"Well, it's no wonder you don't have any friends!" Shrek continued.

Donkey looked at Shrek for a moment, considering these words. For a second, it looked as if he was startled enough to actually shut up. But no. He was Donkey. "Wow!" he said enthusiastically. "Only a true friend could be that cruelly honest."

"Listen, little donkey," said Shrek, looking down at the donkey, whose head came up to about waist-level on the ogre. "Take a look at me. What am I?"

Donkey craned his neck to look up at Shrek's face. "Ahhhh, really tall?" he guessed.

"*No!* I'm an ogre! You know, as in 'grab your torch and pitchforks!' Doesn't that bother you?"

"Nope," replied Donkey.

"Really?" said Shrek, a little surprised.

"Really, really," Donkey assured him, sounding incredibly sincere.

Shrek was suddenly disarmed. He wasn't used to anyone looking deeper than his ugly green skin. "Oh . . . ?"

"Man, I like you. What's your name?" asked Donkey.

" Ahh . . . Shrek," said the ogre hesitantly. Then he turned and continued on his way.

This, finally, almost shut Donkey up. "Shrek?"

he said at last, trying to absorb this unfortunate name. But he was not to be daunted, not even by a name like Shrek. He shook it off. "Well, you know what I like about you, Shrek?" he said. "You got that kind of 'I don't care what anybody thinks of me' thing. I like that, I respect that, Shrek. You're all right."

four
Company

hey had come to the crest of a hill, which sloped down into a large swampy area. Beyond this lay Shrek's house. As Shrek and Donkey started down the winding path, they began passing Shrek's signs: KEEP OUT. STAY AWAY. DANGER.

At last, they came upon Shrek's place. It was not a big place. It was not a lovely place. It was not a home from the pages of *House Beautiful*—but it was all Shrek's. He had put every lump of mud into it himself, made the roof out of sticks and stones he'd gathered from his own swamp.

"Whooh!" said Donkey, unaware of this fact. "Look at that! Who'd want to live in a place like that?"

"Well, I would. That's my home," said Shrek, visibly stung.

Donkey quickly began to backpedal. "Oh, and it is lovely," he gushed. "Just beautiful. You know, you are quite a decorator. It's amazing what you've done with such a modest budget!" He pointed to a large rock in the front yard. "I like that boulder," he enthused. "That is a nice boulder." Shrek just threw him a look as they kept walking toward the house.

Now Donkey noticed the BEWARE OF OGRE signs that were scattered around the property. Once again, he started to feel a little uncomfortable. "I guess you don't entertain much, do you?" he ventured nervously.

"I like my privacy," replied the ogre curtly, looking significantly at his unwanted guest.

"You know, I do too!" Donkey plunged on, missing Shrek's implication entirely. "That's another thing we have in common. Like, I hate it when you got somebody in your face, and you try to give them a hint, and they won't leave, and then there's that big, awkward silence. . . . You know?"

There was a big, awkward silence. . . . Shrek glared at Donkey. Donkey looked worried.

At last, Donkey just decided to spit it out. "Can I stay with you?"

Shrek turned, caught by surprise. "What?" he said. This donkey could not possibly be serious—could he?

"Can I stay with you? Please?"

Shrek smiled at him. "Of course," he said.

"Really?" Donkey said hopefully.

"No."

All else having failed, Donkey resorted to pleading. "*Pleeeeeze!*" he begged. "I don't wanna go back there. You don't know what it's like to be considered a freak! Well, maybe you do. But, that's why we gotta stick together! You've got to let me stay! Please! Please!"

Donkey now climbed up right in Shrek's face, hooves on his chest, totally overwhelming the ogre.

"*Okay!*" yelled Shrek, defeated. "Okay. But—*one night only*."

"Oh, thank you," said Donkey.

Shrek turned and opened his door, shaking his head, whereupon Donkey charged into the mud house.

"No, no, no!" cried the startled ogre. This was not what he'd had in mind at all.

But Donkey was way ahead of him. "Oh, this is gonna be fun. We can stay up late swapping manly stories—and in the morning, I'm makin' *waffles*."

Donkey trotted across the room and jumped up into Shrek's very favorite cushy alligator-skin recliner. Shrek glared at him. *Nobody* sat in that chair. *Ever.* Shrek watched as Donkey turned around in circles until he found just the right position, and then plopped down. He looked quite comfortable.

"Ugh!" muttered the ogre.

"Where do I sleep?" chirped Donkey.

Shrek was too exasperated even to talk. He pointed frantically to the door.

"*Outside!*" he finally spluttered.

Dejected, Donkey climbed down off the lounge chair and headed toward the door. "Oh, ah, I guess that's cool. I mean, I don't know you, and you don't know me, so I guess outside is best." He sniffed, trying to hold back his emotions. "Here I go. Good night."

Donkey sighed a mighty, hurt sigh and walked out the door.

Shrek slammed it behind him. The last thing he saw was Donkey's sad face.

He looked regretfully at the door for a moment, but then he shook it off. Shrek liked his privacy—he didn't need anyone hanging around. Donkey had to go.

Donkey, of course, had still not shut up. Now he was talking right through the door. "I mean," he said, "I do like the outdoors. I'm a donkey. I was born outside. You know I'll just be sittin' by myself. Outside, I guess. You know. By myself. Outside." He began singing to himself: "*I'm all alone. . . . There's no one here beside me. . . .*"

five
Lots More Company

nside the house, Shrek began preparing to dine alone, the way he always dined. The way he liked to dine. He pulled a bit of wax out of his ear to add to his mountainous brown candle. Then he arranged some giant slugs and black fungus in a tasteful pattern on his plate, and plopped an eyeball into his swamp juice martini. There. Perfect. There'd never been a nicer meal on his handmade rottenwood table.

Outside, Donkey lay down on Shrek's doorstep.

A little while later, as Shrek was sitting at the dinner table eating, he heard a noise. It sounded like his door opening. "I thought I told you to stay outside," he called.

"I am outside," Donkey replied from outside.

Now Shrek heard some sort of skittering noise. Okay, so Donkey hadn't opened the door. But somebody had. When he looked up from his bowl, he saw a shadow flit by. He spun around, searching the room, spooked.

Suddenly, there was a crash. Shrek whipped around—and there, stumbling around on his dinner table, were three mice wearing sunglasses, tapping their canes, stumbling blindly about.

Mouse Number One gestured to his tiny compatriots as he spoke, in the process knocking over Shrek's prized jar of eyeballs. "Well, gents," he squeaked, "it's a far cry from the farm, but what choice do we have?"

"It's not home," said Mouse Number Two valiantly, "but it'll do just fine." Then he tripped and fell flat on his face.

Shrek, beginning to recover from the shock of having his privacy invaded, headed toward the table to deal with these little intruders. Meanwhile, Mouse Number Three had discovered Shrek's beloved earwax candle and was sliding down its slippery side. And Mouse Number One had begun to bounce on Shrek's mud slug. "What a lovely bed!" he said.

Shrek lunged for him. "Gotcha!" he cried. But the mouse had already bounced out of his grasp.

Mouse Number Three, meanwhile, had bitten Shrek's ear.

"I've found some cheese!" he reported. Then

he made an awful face and spat it out.

"Blech! Awful stuff!" he cried, jumping onto the table and catapulting a spoonful of gravy into Shrek's eye.

"Is that you, Gordo?" said Mouse Number One, feeling around.

"How did you know?" responded Mouse Number Three, pleasantly surprised.

Shrek had had it. He swooped down and scooped the mice off the dinner table with his huge hand. "Enough!" he bellowed at them. "What are you doing in my house?"

But before he could throw them out, he was hit by something from behind. It was a clear coffin. Startled, he dropped the mice and they escaped—right past the Seven Dwarves, who had just shoved the glass-encased Snow White onto the table.

"Hey!" Shrek yelled. "Oh no, no, no. Dead girl off the table!"

Shrek shoved the coffin back at the dwarves.

"Where are we supposed to put her?" demanded one of them. "The bed's taken!"

"Huh?" Confused, Shrek rushed across the kitchen and pulled open the snakeskin curtain that set off the bedroom, revealing the Big Bad Wolf, dressed in a nightie and resting comfortably in Shrek's bed. Shrek stared at him, dumbfounded.

"What?" said the wolf irritably.

That was it. Shrek grabbed the wolf by the scruff of the neck and dragged him out from under the covers. "I live in a swamp!" he railed. "I put up signs! I'm a terrifying ogre! What do I have to do to get a little *privacy*?"

He carted the wolf to the front door and opened it to throw him out. But outside, a surprise was waiting for him. A very big, bad surprise.

Filling Shrek's swamp, as far as the eye could see, was a teeming sea of unhappy-looking fairy-tale creatures. Big ones, little ones, blue ones, green ones. Refugee tents were everywhere. The Pied Piper was camped with his rats, right next to the Old Lady Who Lived in a Shoe and her brood. Two of the Three Bears huddled around a campfire with several elves. Everywhere, dwarves, fairies, and unicorns, witches and wizards, had grouped around fires. Shrek's jaw hung open as he took in this crowd of uninvited guests—his worst nightmare. "Oh no!" he screamed. "No, no, *nooo!*"

Suddenly, Shrek was further startled by a powerful roar, like the sound of approaching jets. He dove for cover, hitting the dirt as a formation of witches on broomsticks landed like fighter pilots at the edge of the swamp. The airborne hags were guided by an intense elf, who wore ear protectors and waved signal flags.

Shrek rose to his full height, fuming. "*What are*

you doing in my swamp?" he roared at the assembled multitudes.

Desperate to get the creatures off his land, Shrek tried to shoo them away. "All right," he shouted, "get out of here! *All* of you, *move* it! Come on, let's go. No, no, not there!" he shouted as some of them ran into his house.

The effort was futile; there were too many of them, and they were all running around in terror. It was like trying to herd cats.

Finally, Shrek's frustrated glare landed on Donkey.

"Hey, don't look at me!" said Donkey. "I didn't invite them."

Then, out of the swarm stepped Pinocchio. He had been "volunteered" by a shove from behind. "Well, gosh," he said, "no one *invited* us."

Shrek wheeled on him, intent on getting to the bottom of this. "*What?*" he said.

"We were forced to come here," said the puppet-boy, trembling with fear of the ogre.

"By who?" Shrek demanded.

Now one of the Three Little Pigs spoke up. "Lord Farquaad!" he reported. "He huffed, und he puffed, und he—signed an eviction notice."

His brothers nodded in agreement.

"All right," said Shrek. "Who knows where this . . . Farquaad guy is?"

The creatures all looked at him blankly—all except

for Donkey. "Oh, I do!" said Donkey, hopping up and down. "I know where he is!"

Shrek was intent on ignoring him. Donkey meant only trouble. "Does anyone *else* know where to find him? Anyone at all. Anyone?"

They all pointed in different directions. Meanwhile, Donkey continued to leap up into Shrek's line of sight. "Me! Me! Oh! Oh! Pick me! Oh, I know, I know. Me, me!"

Shrek sighed. "Okay, fine," he said.

Then he turned to the crowd. "Attention all . . . fairy-tale things!" he announced loudly.

The creatures fell into an uneasy silence as the ogre continued. "Do *not* get comfortable. Your welcome is officially worn out. In fact, I'm gonna see this guy Farquaad right now, and get you all off my land and back where you came from!"

There was a brief silence as the creatures absorbed this news. Then they erupted into loud cheers. "Yaaaayyyyyy!" they screamed. Like Munchkins surrounding Dorothy, the fairy-tale characters gathered around Shrek to celebrate him as their hero. Birds draped the annoyed ogre in garlands.

Shrek rolled his eyes. Misunderstood again. "Ugh!" he said. Then he pointed at Donkey. "You! You're coming with me."

Delighted to be included, Donkey stamped his feet in glee. "All right, that's what I like to hear, man!

Shrek and Donkey, two stalwart friends off on a whirl-wind, big city adventure. I love it!"

As Shrek started down the road in search of Farquaad, Donkey caught up to him and danced alongside him. He was very happy. Shrek was very grouchy.

But Donkey didn't notice Shrek's bad mood. "*On the road again,*" he sang as they left the swamp behind. "Sing it with me, Shrek. . . ."

"What did I say about singing?" said Shrek.

"Well, can I whistle?"

"No."

"Well, can I hum it?"

"All right," said the ogre. "Humming."

And off they went, walking into the woods—a humming donkey and his new friend, the ogre.

six
Farquaad Picks a Wife

lsewhere in the kingdom, in a dungeon in the gloomy depths of Farquaad's castle, a tall glass of cold milk was being poured by a burly, hooded torturer.

Farquaad entered the chamber and stood behind the torturer, watching the man perform his ominous task. Farquaad was a rather strange-looking fellow, with an enormous chin and an unflattering page-boy hairdo. The fact that he was only about four-and-a-half-feet tall just made the whole effect look more peculiar.

In the torturer's hand was a cookie, which he began dunking repeatedly into the milk, holding it under the surface for excruciating moments at a time.

Though Farquaad could not see the victim, he knew just who it was. It was the Gingerbread Man.

"No!!! Ahhhh! Bbbblbbblbbbl," spluttered the hapless victim.

"That's enough," said Farquaad. "He's ready to talk."

The torturer stepped aside, revealing the coughing, hacking Gingerbread Man lying helplessly on a baking tray, surrounded by spatters of milk.

Farquaad strode up to the torturer's table. Because he was such a tiny fellow, however, his stride was quite short. And when he stood beside the table, only the top of his big red hat was visible above the edge.

"Heh heh heh heh heh," laughed Farquaad menacingly. Then he cleared his throat. The effect of his menacing laugh was not quite as powerful as it might have been, since the Gingerbread Man could not see him. Farquaad did not look pleased.

Two guards rushed forward to lower the table mechanically. There, that was better. Farquaad now towered—slightly—above the victim. "Run, run, run as fast as you can," Farquaad taunted him, picking up his little flat legs and playing with them. "You can't catch me—I'm the Gingerbread Man!"

"You're a monster!" the Gingerbread Man managed to choke out.

"I'm not the monster here, you are," Farquaad responded. "You and the rest of that fairy-tale trash poisoning my perfect world. Now, tell me, where are the others?"

"Eat me!" retorted the valiant little gingerbread man, spitting a mouthful of milk into Farquaad's face.

Farquaad slowly wiped the milk off. "I've tried to be fair to you creatures," he said through clenched teeth, "but now my patience has reached its end. Tell me or I'll . . ." He leaned over, reaching for the Gingerbread Man's buttons.

"No! Not the buttons," pleaded the agitated cookie. "Not my gumdrop buttons!"

"All right, then, who's hiding them?" Farquaad wanted to know.

The Gingerbread Man was a broken cookie. "Okay . . . I'll tell you. Do you know the Muffin Man?" he said tonelessly.

"The Muffin Man?" Farquaad echoed.

"The Muffin Man."

"Yes. I know the Muffin Man," said Farquaad. "Who lives on Drury Lane?"

"Well," said the Gingerbread Man, "she's married to the Muffin Man."

"The Muffin Man?"

"The Muffin Man!" screamed the Gingerbread Man, unable to take it any longer.

Farquaad turned away. "She's married to the Muffin Man . . ." he said to himself, thoughtfully.

The dungeon doors burst open suddenly and a guard approached Farquaad. "My lord, we found it," he reported.

Immediately, Farquaad forgot all about the Muffin Man's wife.

"What are you waiting for?" he cried eagerly. "Bring it in!"

A shrouded figure, hanging from a chain, was brought before Farquaad. He looked at it with greedy anticipation..

Whoosh! The guards pulled the cover off, revealing the thing that Farquaad was so excited about. It was a large, ornately framed mirror. A serious face appeared on its silver surface.

"Ahhhhh," said the guards, admiringly.

"Ohhh," said the Gingerbread Man, knowing this meant trouble.

"Magic Mirror," Farquaad began in awe.

"*Don't tell him anything!*" the Gingerbread Man shrieked from the cookie sheet where he lay.

Farquaad reached out his foot and stepped on the pedal of a flip-top garbage can. The metal lid sprang up, and Farquaad violently swiped the Gingerbread Man from the table into the garbage. "No!" screamed the Gingerbread Man. "Ahh!!!" But his cries were cut short by the lid as it banged shut over him.

Now Farquaad turned his full attention to the Magic Mirror. He smiled ominously. "Evening!" he said brightly.

He stepped toward the mirror. "Mirror, mirror, on the wall," he said, "is this not the most perfect kingdom of them all?"

"Well, technically," said the mirror, "you're not a king."

"Thelonious . . ." Farquaad called out.

Thelonious, the muscular guard in the scary hood, approached the mirror. He held up a small hand mirror and, with one sharp punch, shattered it.

The magic mirror caught on very quickly. It had made a mistake, a big one.

"What I mean," it said, scrambling to recover, "is you're not a king yet. But you can become one. All you have to do is marry a princess."

"Go on," said Farquaad as Thelonious hovered menacingly over the mirror.

"Aaannnddd . . ." said the mirror, nervously playing for time, "I can find you the perfect princess."

When it saw the grin beginning to spread on Farquaad's face, the mirror loosened up a little. Things were going to be okay. In fact, it was time to have a little fun.

"So just sit back and relax, my lord," said the mirror, snapping into the upbeat voice of a game show host, "because it's time for you to meet today's eligible bachelorettes, and . . . here they are!" As bouncy game-show music magically kicked in, the mirror gestured to one side, revealing three shadowy portraits of princesses.

"Bachelorette Number One," said the mirror in the same cheesy game-show voice, "is a mentally abused shut-in from a kingdom far, far away. She likes sushi and hot-tubbing anytime! Her hobbies include cooking and cleaning for her two evil sisters! Please welcome . . . Cinderella!"

The lights came up on the first silhouette, and there she was, in all her forlorn beauty.

But the mirror was still talking, really getting into it now. "Bachelorette Number Two," it said, "is a cape-wearing girl from the land of fancy. Although she lives with seven other men, she's not easy! Just kiss her dead, frozen lips and find out what a live wire she is! Come on, give it up for Snow White!"

A light popped on to highlight a portrait of Snow White.

"And last," concluded the mirror, "but certainly not least, Bachelorette Number Three is a fiery red-head from a dragon-guarded castle, surrounded by hot boiling lava! But don't let that cool you off. She's a loaded pistol who likes piña coladas and getting caught in the rain. Yours for the rescuing . . . *Princess Fiona!*"

The third light popped on, revealing a portrait of a breathtakingly beautiful princess with flaming red hair.

"So will it be Bachelorette Number One, Bachelorette Number Two, or Bachelorette Number Three?" said the mirror.

The game show crowd, comprised of the guards, immediately began to shout out their favorite numbers. "One!" "Three!" "Two!" "Three!" "One!" "Two!" "Three!" "One!" "Two!"

Farquaad was in a tizzy. "One," he said hesitantly. "Two. Three. Um, One. Three. Um . . ."

"Three," said Thelonious, holding up two fingers. "Pick Three."

Farquaad kept waffling, overcome by his incredible choices. "One, Two, Three, um, One, Three, um, well . . . okay, okay, Number Three!"

"Lord Farquaad," announced the mirror officiously, "you've chosen . . . Princess Fiona!"

Immediately, there was wild applause from the guards. Farquaad was ecstatic, captivated by the portrait of Fiona. Then he turned away, lost in thought. "Princess Fiona," he said dreamily. "She's perfect. All I have to do," he mused, "is just find someone to go . . ."

The mirror interrupted his little reverie. "But I probably should *mention* the little thing that happens at night when . . ."

"That's it," said Farquaad, not listening to the mirror in the least. He was too busy formulating his big plan.

"Yes," the mirror tried again, "but after sunset . . ."

"Silence!" thundered Farquaad. "I will make this Princess Fiona *my queen*, and DuLoc will finally have the perfect king!" He snapped his fingers at a knight. "Captain," he ordered, "assemble your finest men. We're going to have a tournament!"

seven
DuLoc Is a Perfect Place

ome time later, Shrek and Donkey emerged from the cornfield by the gates of DuLoc. They gazed up at Farquaad's castle, which consisted of a single tall tower looming above the center of the city.

"Well that's it, that's it right there," said Donkey smugly. "That's DuLoc. I told you I'd find it."

"So that must be Lord Farquaad's castle?" Shrek said in distaste as he headed toward the gate, taking great ogre strides.

"Hey wait, wait up, Shrek!" called Donkey, taking off after him. Shrek was now passing through a parking lot that was dotted with wooden carts. All over the lot were tall signs that read, YOU ARE PARKED IN LANCELOT XVII, or YOU ARE PARKED IN PERCIVAL XII.

Donkey caught up with Shrek, breathless, just as they reached the entrance to Farquaad's kingdom. There they found a velvet rope that was hung in a maze for crowd control. The maze was totally empty. Standing next to it was a man wearing a giant fake Farquaad head. The sign beside him read, 45 MINUTE WAIT FROM HERE.

"Hey . . . you!" Shrek called, unsure of what to make of this figure. "Where can I find Lord Farquaad?"

"Ahhhhhhh!" shrieked the man from inside the head. He began to run from Shrek, zigging back and forth between the velvet ropes.

Shrek was irritated. "Wait a second. Hello," he said. "Look, I'm not gonna eat ya. I just . . . I just . . ."

But it was no use. The man, still screaming in terror and weaving his way through the rope maze, proceeded to crash into one of the poles, knocking himself out cold. Shrek sighed in exasperation.

Meanwhile, Donkey started trotting obediently through the maze of velvet ropes. Back and forth, up and down. Shrek watched in bemusement, and then lumbered right through, knocking down the whole maze.

At the far end, blocking the entrance, was a turnstile. Shrek went through, and Donkey followed. Or at least, Donkey tried to. But the turnstile was not made for four-legged creatures. No matter how hard he tried, he kept getting stuck. With one final push, Donkey managed to get his whole body into the turnstile. It spun him upside down, then spat him out on the ground next to Shrek. Once out, he jumped to all fours, and followed Shrek into the square.

They stopped and looked around. What kind of kingdom was this? It was insanely orderly, with perfect lines of neat cone-shaped trees, grass that looked as if it had been cut with an electric shaver, and rows of houses that were all exactly the same. Chirpy music was being piped in from somewhere. Nearby, a booth featured Farquaad souvenir figurines. The place was deserted.

Shrek sniffed the air. "It's quiet," he said. "Too quiet. Where is everybody?"

Donkey had spotted an information booth down the street a bit. On the side was a large handle that said PULL.

"Hey, look at this," he said, rushing over to it and pulling the lever. The device started to click, and then it clunked into action. The doors on the front of the booth flew open, revealing rows of perfect little wooden dolls, who immediately started to sing:

> *Welcome to DuLoc, such a perfect town.*
> *Here we have some rules, let us lay them down.*
> *Don't make waves, stay in line.*
> *And we'll get along fine.*

DuLoc is a perfect place.
Please keep off of the grass.
Shine your shoes, wipe your . . . face.
DuLoc is, DuLoc is, DuLoc is a perfect place.

Donkey and Shrek stood staring at the display, dumbstruck expressions on their faces.

Then there was a bright flash, and an instant photo of them—capturing their befuddled looks—was spat out of the machine.

Slam! The doors closed. Donkey and Shrek stood there for a moment, still a little stunned.

Then Donkey grinned. "Wow! Let's do that again!" he said.

But Shrek had other ideas. "No!" he yelled. "No! No. No, no . . . no." He was here to get his swamp back. The last thing he needed was to see that ridiculous song-and-dance number again.

Shrek and Donkey walked on toward the center of DuLoc. Here they spotted a stadium, and an entrance to a tunnel that led into it. A noise seemed to be coming from the far end of the tunnel. They went in and began walking through the half-dark, not knowing what they would find at the other end. Dimly, they could see a light far ahead.

As Shrek and his companion walked along, Donkey loudly began to hum the "Welcome to DuLoc" tune.

"All right," Shrek warned him, "you're going the right way for a smacked bottom!"

"Sorry about that."

Now they could hear the sounds of a trumpet fanfare and a crowd cheering. Faintly, the sound of a voice began to reach them. It was Farquaad's voice, and he was declaiming loudly to what they could hear was a large, cheering crowd.

"Brave knights!" shouted Farquaad. "You are the best and the brightest in all the land, and today one of you shall prove himself better and brighter than all the rest."

They kept walking, the cheering getting louder as they moved ahead. At last, they reached the end. They emerged into a brilliant light, the packed stadium stretching out before them. Little Lord Farquaad stood on a high podium, basking in the applause of his people.

Farquaad continued to address the crowd. "That champion," he proclaimed, "shall have the honor— no, no, the *privilege*—to go forth and rescue the lovely Princess Fiona from the fiery keep of the dragon. If, for any reason, the winner is unsuccessful, the first runner-up will take his place, and so on and so forth. Some of you may die, but it's a sacrifice I am willing to make." Shrek looked around in amazement. Yes, the people were applauding, but they had a little help: Farquaad had guards stationed all over the stadium, holding up cue cards to the crowd. CHEERS, the cards read, and APPLAUSE.

Farquaad threw up his arms grandly. "Let the tournament begin!" he hollered.

Between Shrek and Farquaad stood a brigade of knights. But Shrek didn't care. He marched forward, and the perfect rows of knights parted in shock before the ogre.

Face to face with Farquaad, Shrek stood defiantly. Next to him, Donkey imitated the defiant stance as best he could. The crowd gasped.

Farquaad started in horror at the sight of this intruder. "What is *that*? " he whined. "Ugh—it's hideous!"

Shrek looked annoyed, but quickly recovered. "Now, that's not very nice!" he admonished. He pointed to his companion. "It's just a donkey."

Farquaad didn't appreciate the joke. "Indeed," he said. He was in no mood to fool around.

Then he got a bright idea. "Knights!" he said. "New plan. The one who kills the ogre will be named champion! Have at him!"

Every warrior turned toward Shrek, whose eyes widened. He backed up as the warriors started toward him, drawing their weapons. "Oh, hey now, come on, hang on now," he said. Backing up into a serving table that stood in front of several huge kegs of ale, Shrek lifted a large mug of beer from the table. "Can't we settle this over a pint?" he said.

The warriors continued to advance, brandishing their weapons.

"No?" Shrek asked them sarcastically. Then he got serious. "All right, then, *Come on!*" he shouted.

As the warriors surged forward with various battle cries, Shrek took a fortifying swig of beer, and then whirled suddenly and knocked the spigots off the kegs with his mug. Instantly, geysers of ale shot out of the kegs, knocking over the knights and soaking into the dirt, turning it into mud. The warriors started slipping and sliding, unable to get their footing, their legs going out from under them.

Shrek smiled contentedly and skated through the mud field like a hockey player. This was fun! After all, ogres and mud went together just like peaches and cream. All around him, the knights struggled in the mud while Shrek grinned.

By now, the area where the horses were usually penned had become a virtual pro wrestling match. As the mayhem continued, the crowd began to root for Shrek, who'd entered the ring and begun performing wrestling moves on the knights. Power slams! Knee bashes! Ankle submission holds! Choke lifts! Pile drivers, using Donkey as the basher! This was a riot.

Donkey joined in for good measure. "Hey, Shrek! Tag me! Tag me!" he called.

Shrek tagged Donkey, and then held a knight while

Donkey head-butted him. The crowd erupted into cheers.

"The chair! Give him the chair!" screamed an old lady.

Shrek crashed a folding chair over a downed knight. He scooped another one up an threw him down in a classic body slam, then turned and delivered a wicked pile driver to another. Donkey, meanwhile, scampered around the ring tossing out head butts and nasty kicks wherever he could get them in. One by one, they eliminated all of the competition as the crowd went wild. Finally, Shrek and Donkey flexed triumphantly for the ecstatic crowd.

"Thank you, I'm Shrek—an ogre-night success!" he said. "Thank you, thank you very much. I'm here till Thursday, try the veal."

Farquaad simply watched, intrigued. He nodded, and suddenly Shrek was surrounded by archers, their arrows trained on him.

"Shall I give the order, sir?" a guard asked him.

"No. I have a better idea," Farquaad replied. Then he turned to the crowd. "People of DuLoc!" he announced, sweeping his arms toward Shrek. "I give you our champion!"

The people cheered louder for Shrek, who was suddenly not sure what to make of all this.

Farquaad was really pleased with his new plan. "Congratulations, ogre!" he said, beaming. "You've won the honor of embarking on a great and noble quest!"

Shrek was now sure he didn't like the way things were going. He was not having any of this. "Quest? I'm already on a quest," he told Farquaad. "A quest to get my swamp back!" He started threateningly toward the podium.

"Your swamp?" Farquaad asked, interested.

"Yeah, my swamp where you dumped those fairy-tale creatures," said Shrek.

"Indeed," said Farquaad. This was all working out very, very nicely. "All right, ogre, I'll make you a deal," he offered suavely. "Go on this quest for me and I'll give you your swamp back."

"Exactly the way it was?" Shrek asked suspiciously.

"Down to the last slime-covered toadstool."

"And the squatters?"

"As good as gone," Farquaad promised.

Shrek considered this new twist for a moment, weighing his options. He narrowed his eyes. "What kind of quest?" he asked.

eight
Layers

nd that was how Shrek and Donkey came to be walking through a sunflower-filled field the very next day.

"Okay, let me get this straight," Donkey was saying. "You're gonna go fight a dragon and rescue a princess, just so Farquaad will give you back your swamp, which you only don't have 'cause he filled it full of freaks in the first place. Is that about right?"

Shrek was already tired of Donkey. "You, know, you're really quite annoying," he said.

They walked on together, Shrek now munching on an onion he had picked up along the way.

"I don't get it, Shrek," said Donkey. "Why didn't you just pull some of that ogre stuff? Like, throttle him, lay siege to his fortress, grind his bones to make your bread—you know, the whole ogre trip."

"Oh—or I know what," said Shrek sarcastically, used to ogre stereotypes by now. "Maybe I could've decapitated an entire village and put their heads on a pike. Gotten a knife, cut open their spleens, and drank their fluids. Does that sound good to you?"

"Ahh . . . no, not really, no," said Donkey, chastened.

"For *your* information, there's a lot more to *ogres* than people think."

"Example?" said Donkey helpfully.

"Example. Okay . . . um . . ." Then Shrek noticed the onion he was still carrying, and a lightbulb went off in his mind. "Ogres," he said, "are like onions."

Donkey sniffed the onion. "They stink?"

"Yes. No!" cried Shrek, all confused.

"Oh!" Donkey offered. "They make you cry."

"No!"

"Oh, I know!" Donkey went on excitedly. "You leave them out in the sun and they get all brown and start sprouting little white hairs."

"No!" Shrek hollered. "Layers. Onions have layers. Ogres have layers. Onions have layers—you get it? We both have layers!"

"Oh," said Donkey, not getting it at all. "You both have layers, oh." Then he sniffed the onion. "You know, not everybody likes onions," he told Shrek. He thought about this problem for a moment. And then he had it. "Cake!" he said happily. "Everybody loves cakes! Cakes have layers."

"I don't care what everyone likes! Ogres are not like cakes."

"You know what else everybody likes?" said Donkey, not easily deterred. "Parfaits. Have you ever met a person and, you say, 'Hey, let's get some parfaits,' and they say, 'Heck, no, I don't like parfaits?' Parfaits are *delicious*."

"No, you dense, irritating, miniature beast of burden!" Shrek roared, feeling really frustrated with Donkey's incessant babbling. "Ogres are like onions! End of story, bye-bye, see ya later."

He stalked off, leaving Donkey momentarily speechless. But only momentarily.

"Parfaits," stated Donkey, running after Shrek, "may be the most delicious thing on the whole planet."

Shrek was way beyond exasperation. "You know what?" he spluttered. "Maybe there's a good reason why donkeys shouldn't talk."

"Do you have a tissue or something?" asked Donkey in blithe cluelessness as they continued down the road. "'Cause I'm making a mess. Just the *word* 'parfait' makes me start slobbering."

Shrek just sighed and kept walking.

After some time, the scenery began to change in a bad way. Little by little, the greenery turned browner, the grass got sparser, until finally Shrek and Donkey found themselves moving across a bleak, burnt landscape marked only by charred skeletons of trees.

Donkey sniffed the air, wrinkling his nose as he took in a particularly unsavory smell. "Whew! Shrek!" he said. "Did you do that? Man! You gotta warn somebody before you just crack one off! My mouth was open and everything."

"Believe me, Donkey, if it was me you'd be dead." Shrek stopped and sniffed. "It's brimstone," he said. "We must be getting close."

"Yeah, right . . . brimstone. Don't be talking about brimstone. I know what I smell and it wasn't brimstone," he said, looking at Shrek's rear end. "It didn't come off of any stone either."

As they continued walking, it began to get darker. Black clouds scudded across the sky, giving the landscape a foreboding feeling. The burned trees cast long, strange shadows across the ground. And just ahead of them, rising up like some kind of monster, was a huge devil's peak.

This was not a nice place.

Nevertheless, there was nothing to do but press on. And that meant climbing the rocky peak, which was no easy feat.

Finally, after hours of climbing, they pulled themselves up over the highest ridge.

And there it was: the Dragon's Keep. It towered before them, a dilapidated castle, burned and blackened. Perched on a rock pinnacle, it was surrounded by a terrifying lake of molten lava.

nine
The Fiery Dragon

hrek tried to make light of it. "Sure, it's big enough," he said. "But look at the location. Heh, heh, heh." With that unconvincing laugh, he struck off toward a wobbly looking wooden bridge that hung high above the bubbling moat. The bridge was the only way to get into the castle.

When they reached the bridge, Donkey suddenly found himself face to face with a horse skull that was impaled on one of the bridge's supports. Now thoroughly scared out of his wits, he hurried past it. He stared fearfully at the huge drop below the bridge, and then trotted miserably after Shrek. "Uh, Shrek," he said as he followed, "ah, remember when you, ah, said that ogres have layers?"

"Yeah," Shrek answered unsurely, not knowing where Donkey was going with this.

"Well . . . I have a bit of a confession to make. Um, donkeys don't have layers. We, we wear our fear right out there on our sleeves."

"Wait a second, donkeys don't have sleeves," said Shrek.

Donkey caught up with Shrek at the foot of the bridge. "You know what I mean," he said.

"Oh! You can't tell me you're afraid of heights," said Shrek. If there was one thing a donkey was supposed to be, it was not afraid of heights.

Donkey peered tentatively over the edge. "No," he said, trying to keep his teeth from chattering, "I'm just a little uncomfortable about being on a rickety bridge over a boiling lake of lava!"

"Come on, Donkey, I'm right here beside you, okay, for emotional support," said Shrek, faking his best encouraging voice. "We'll just tackle this thing together, one little baby step at a time."

"Really?"

"Really. Really."

"Okay, that makes me feel so much better," said Donkey, looking just as terrified as before.

With Shrek right behind him, Donkey stepped gingerly out onto the bridge and started to pick his way among the flimsy slats.

"Just keep moving and don't look down," said Shrek.

"Don't look down. Don't look down," chanted Donkey. "Keep on moving and don't look down. . . . Don't look down, keep on moving, and don't look down." Little by little, Donkey moved forward. He was doing well, too, until he stepped on a loose slat, which gave way and plummeted into the boiling moat below.

As Donkey fell forward, he couldn't help but see through the opening. "Shrek? *I'm looking down!*" he said, spinning around in a panic. "Arggghhhh! I can't do this. Just let me off right now, please!"

Shrek was starting to get irritated. "But you're already halfway," he said.

"Yeah, but I know *that* half is safe," retorted Donkey, pointing to the half of the bridge he'd already traversed.

"Okay, fine!" said the ogre. "I don't have time for this. You go back." He tried to get past Donkey, but the bridge was too narrow. And as they struggled, the bridge began to shake and sway.

"Shrek! No. Wait!" yelled Donkey, as the bridge moved beneath him.

"I can't get past you. Donkey, you go left, I'll go right. Let's have a dance then, shall we?" said the ogre, shaking the bridge a little more just to annoy Donkey.

"Ahh! Don't do that!" shrieked Donkey, jumping back over the missing board. He leaped back away from Shrek, in the direction Shrek wanted him to go—across the bridge.

"Oh, I'm sorry—do what? Oh—this?" said Shrek, swinging the bridge even harder.

"Yes! That!"

"Yes? Yes, do it? Okay!" Shrek now started shaking the bridge violently, causing Donkey to back farther across in terror. The ogre was doing exactly what he intended to do: propelling the hysterical donkey backward, step by step, to the other end.

"No! Shrek! Shrek! No. Stop it!" Donkey screeched.

"But you just said do it, and I'm doin' it!" Shrek laughed over Donkey's pleas.

"Oh, God, I'm gonna die, I'm gonna die. Shrek, I'm gonna die," screamed Donkey. And as he screamed, eyes closed, he continued to back up, unaware that he had almost crossed the bridge.

His eyes popped open, and he found that he was looking down at solid ground.

"Oh!" he gasped.

Shrek leaned over and gently patted Donkey on the cheek. "That'll do, Donkey. That'll do," he said softly.

Donkey looked back over the bridge. "Cool!" he said. Now that he wasn't going to die, he was back to his old self.

He followed Shrek toward the enormous castle doors. They were completely unguarded; obviously the dragon hadn't expected anybody to make it over the shaky bridge above the boiling lava.

"So," said Donkey with newfound confidence, "where is this fire-breathin' pain in the neck anyway?"

"Inside, waiting for us to rescue her," Shrek replied.

"I was talking about the dragon, Shrek."

They slipped in the door, and the two of them started making their way through the murky hallways of the dragon's dark and spooky keep. Not knowing what he might find inside, Shrek was wary. Donkey was downright terrified. Only an occasional glittering torch lit the gloom. The passages were littered with bones of unknown origin, large and small, and also with random pieces of armor.

"Hey, Shrek," Donkey whispered, trying to hide the fear in his voice. "You afraid?"

"No," said Shrek in a normal voice. "But—SHHHHHHH!"

The startled donkey jumped a mile. "Oh, good—me neither," he said in a trembling voice. Then he heard a noise from somewhere in the castle. "Aaagh!" he screamed.

"Well," he continued, trying to regain his composure, "of course, there's nothing wrong with being afraid. You know, fear's a sensible response to an unfamiliar situation. An unfamiliar, *dangerous* situation, I might add—and with a dragon that breathes fire and eats knights and breathes fire . . . it sure doesn't mean you're a coward if you're a little scared, you know what I mean? 'Cause I sure as heck ain't no coward, I know that."

Suddenly, Donkey fell into a pile of knight bones and armor. "Ahhhhh!" he screamed as a helmet tumbled onto his head.

Shrek removed the helmet and put it onto his own head just to try out the look. Then he turned to his companion. "Donkey?" he said. "Two things, okay? Shut. Up." He counted the words off on his fingers. Then he pointed to the left. "Now go over there and see if you can find any stairs."

"Stairs? I thought we were looking for the princess!"

"The princess will be up the stairs, in the highest room, in the tallest tower."

"What makes you think she'll be there?"

"I read it in a book once," said Shrek, walking away.

"Cool," said Donkey, looking as courageous as possible. "You handle the dragon, I'll handle the stairs."

Shrek headed off down the corridor. Donkey watched him go, then moved off the other way. "Oh, I'll find those stairs," he muttered to himself. "I'll whup their behind, too. That's right. Those stairs won't know which way they're going. Gonna take drastic steps. Kick 'em to the curb. Don't mess with me, I'm the stair master, I've mastered the stairs. I wish

I had a step right here, right here, now—I'd step all over it." He was so busy talking, he didn't notice a huge eye, just watching him as he climbed the stairs.

Shrek, meanwhile, had reached the other end of the corridor. Through a window, he could now see a slender tower wrapped in a staircase. It was connected to the keep by a stone walkway. "Oh, well I bet that's where the princess is," he said to himself. "But where's the—

"*Dragon! Ahhhhhhh!*" Donkey screamed, having just found himself eyeball to eyeball with the aforementioned creature.

Maybe Donkey was the stair master, but he was definitely not the dragon master. He did the prudent thing: he ran away, screaming. "Whaaaaa!" he yelled, just managing to dodge a huge fireball.

Down at the end of the hall, Shrek turned to see Donkey headed for him at a gallop, the fireball hurtling along right behind him. "Donkey! Look out!" Shrek yelled as Donkey raced past.

Shrek grabbed Donkey and just managed to jump out of the fireball's way, dragging Donkey with him. Then they started running.

They made for the tall tower, which looked like the nearest place to take cover. But a moment later they were shooting out again, Donkey leading the way, another fireball right behind them. Shrek leaped to one side and let the fireball rocket past. Donkey, meanwhile, kept running, back onto the walkway. The fireball was right behind him. Just as it was about to catch him, he dropped to the floor and flattened himself down as hard as he could. "Now I lay me down to sleep," he prayed, "I hope I live another week." The fireball roared over him, just singeing the tuft of his tail.

But Donkey wasn't out of the woods yet, because now the dragon was coming after him, roaring ferociously. Shrek quickly scrambled up the stairs on the tower and took a flying leap off the top, landing squarely on the dragon's huge tail.

"Gotcha!" he yelled.

This fight was a long way from over, though. The dragon simply whipped its tail back and forth, sending Shrek hurtling through the air and crashing right through the roof of the tower. He landed on the stone floor of a bedchamber, only half-conscious.

Outside, the dragon was just getting going. Now it was using its tail to smash through the raised walkway like a wrecking ball, cutting off Donkey's escape route.

"Whoaaaa!" yelled Donkey as the huge tail cut through the walkway again, right in front of him.

"Whaaa, wup, wooo!" he yelled as he ran back and forth, trying to find a place on the bridge to cling to.

Finally, Donkey was trapped atop a single supporting column. The dragon closed in, its menacing silhouette looming through the smoke.

"No . . . Don't . . ." pleaded Donkey as the dragon's gigantic head moved closer and closer. "Oh, no—oh—oh, what large teeth you have!" he blurted. It didn't matter what he said, he was going to die anyway.

Curious, the dragon growled and glared. It moved even closer to Donkey, who was desperately searching his mind for something else to say that might keep the dragon from french frying him.

"I mean—white, sparkling teeth!" he chattered frantically.

The dragon paused, looked at him inquisitively, and then smiled. Donkey immediately seized the opportunity. He was on to something here with this thing about the teeth; he just had to play it right.

"I know you probably hear this all the time from your food," he said, "but you must bleach or something 'cause that is one dazzling smile you've got there. And do I detect a hint of minty freshness?"

The dragon smiled and peered at Donkey. It was wary, but clearly intrigued.

"And you know what else?" vamped Donkey, really warming up to it now, "You know what else? You're—"

The dragon leaned toward him and gazed adorably.

Suddenly it was all clear to Donkey. "—a *girl* dragon! Uh-oh . . . I mean, of *course* you're a girl dragon! 'Cause you're just reeking of feminine beauty."

The dragon batted her eyelashes, which were rather long.

"What's the matter with you, you got something in your eye?" said Donkey, not quite getting the message.

The dragon blew a heart-shaped smoke ring.

Now Donkey got the message. "Hey, oh," he said. "Oh, man, I'd really love to stay but I'm an asthmatic and I don't know if it'll work out if you're going to be blowing smoke rings and stuff—" He coughed significantly.

The dragon just purred and lifted Donkey by his tail. She carried him off to her lair. She was smitten.

"Shrek! Help!" screamed Donkey. "No! No! No! Shrek! Shrek!"

ten
A Shrek in Shining Armor

p in the tower, Shrek lay on the floor where he had landed, a bit dazed. He was still wearing the knight's helmet he'd put on earlier. Behind him, on a bed near the window, lay Princess Fiona, her gorgeous red hair set off perfectly by an emerald-green dress.

Unseen by Shrek, the princess peeked over at him and saw what appeared to be a knight struggling to his feet.

Lying prettily on her canopy bed, she awaited her knight in shining armor. She waited. Nothing happened. Then, on second thought, she leaned over, grabbed a bouquet of flowers, clutched it to her breast, and resumed her Sleeping Beauty pose.

Finally, Shrek made it to his feet. His visor lowered, he crossed the room to the bed where Fiona lay.

Fiona, still pretending to be asleep, puckered her lips slightly. She was ready. But instead of giving her a kiss, Shrek bent over her, grabbed her by the shoulders, and shook her.

"Wha, wha . . ." said Fiona. This was not how it was supposed to work!

"Wake up!" Shrek commanded.

"What?" she snapped angrily.

"Are you Princess Fiona?"

"I am," she replied, recovering. "Awaiting a knight so bold as to rescue me."

"Ah, that's nice," said Shrek brusquely, wanting nothing to do with her helpless princess routine. "Now, let's go."

As Shrek turned to leave, Fiona sat bolt upright. "But wait, Sir Knight!" she said desperately. Then she made as graceful a flourish as she could under her flustered circumstances. "This be-eth our first meeting," she said. "Should it not be a wonderful, romantic moment?"

Shrek walked back to Fiona, grabbed her by the arm, and hauled her out of bed. "Yeah, sorry, lady. C'mon, there's no time."

"Hey, wait! What are you doing?" she protested as

he dragged her across the room. Finding that the door was locked, he jiggled the handle impatiently.

"You know you should sweep me off my feet," Fiona instructed, "out yonder window and down a rope onto your valiant steed!"

"You've had a lot of time to plan this, haven't you?" said Shrek dryly.

"Uh-huh," replied the princess.

Then he threw his shoulder against the door, which flew open. Shrek crashed through, dragging Fiona behind him.

"Argggh! Ugh!" she said. Then she collected herself and tried again, even though she was running to keep up with him as he pulled her along by the arm. "We have to savor this moment! You could . . . recite an epic poem for me? A ballad? A sonnet? A limerick?" Finally she jerked herself free. "Or something!" she concluded.

"I don't think so," said Shrek.

They stopped for a moment as Shrek tried to figure out which direction to go.

"Well, can I at least know the name of my champion?" asked Fiona, thoroughly fed up.

"Um . . . Shrek," said the ogre, who was preoccupied with trying to figure which way was out.

Fiona produced a handkerchief. "Sir Shrek," she said haltingly. It was not quite as glamorous a name as she'd hoped for. She cleared her throat. "I pray that you will take this favor as a token of my gratitude."

Shrek regarded the cloth curiously, and then wiped his sooty brow with it, completely blackening it. He handed it back to Fiona. "Thanks," he said.

Fiona stared at the handkerchief. But before could react, she was startled by an enormous roar from the dragon.

"You didn't slay the dragon?" asked Fiona, shocked. This guy was really not playing by the rules.

"It's on my to-do list. Now, c'mon!" He grabbed her arm and hauled her around a corner and down a flight of stairs.

"But this isn't right!" Fiona protested, stumbling along behind him. "You're meant to charge in, sword drawn, banner flying! That's what all the other knights did."

Shrek pointed to a skeleton that lay slumped near the doorway, a charred outline of a man burned into the stone behind it. "Yeah. Right before they burst into flames," he said.

Fiona pulled free from Shrek and stopped running, indignant. Shrek just kept on going. He was heading toward the hall where he had left Donkey.

"You know that's not the point!" she said. Then she stopped short in surprise. "Ugh! Wait—where are you going?" she demanded, pointing in the other direction. "The exit's over there!"

"Well, I have to save my ass!" Shrek called back to her over his shoulder. He meant Donkey, of course, but Fiona didn't know that.

"Ahhh!" she shrieked. "What kind of knight *are* you?"

But Shrek just kept going, opening the door carefully. "One of a kind," he called back to her.

eleven
True Love's First Kiss

 onkey, it seemed, had gotten himself into something of a situation. When Shrek opened the door to the dragon's chamber, he was greeted by an amazing sight. There was the dragon, sitting atop an enormous pile of gems and jewels that glittered like a disco light show. And there was Donkey, held fast in the dragon's coiled tail, desperately trying to talk his way out of the night of romance she was happily preparing. She had already lit a candelabra over her head and drawn the curtains.

"Slow down, slow, baby, slow down, slow down, baby, please. Look, I believe it's healthy to get to know someone, over, you know, a long time. I mean, just call me old-fashioned, you know. I don't want to rush into a physical relationship. Uh, I'm not, ah, emotionally ready for a commitment of, ah, this, ah, magnitude," babbled Donkey.

Ignoring his protests, the dragon dreamily caressed Donkey under his chin with her huge claw. "Hey " he yelped. "That is unwanted physical contact "

As amusing as this scene was, Shrek knew he had to rescue Donkey. Looking around for an opportunity, he spied the chain that led up to the candelabra. Donkey, not seeing Shrek, was still trying to play for time, hoping for a miracle. "*Hey!* What are you doing?!" he squealed. "Okay, okay, okay. Look—let's just back up a little and take this one step at a time. I mean, we really should get to know each other first. You know, as, as friends, or maybe even as pen pals. You know, 'cause I'm on the road a lot, but I just love receiving cards—"

The dragon licked him, slurping her huge tongue up the side of his face.

"Oh! Hey!" he cried. "You know, I, I'd really love to stay, but—Hey! Hey! Don't do that!" Donkey cried as he felt the dragon stroke his tail between her long talons. "That's my tail, that's my personal tail, you're gonna tear it off! I don't give permission to . . ."

Unnoticed by both the dragon and Donkey, Shrek swung down on the chain and reached out to grab Donkey. But he was way too high. He swung backward and forward until he came to a stop directly above Donkey. Then he looked up and found that the chain was jammed above him. He started shaking it to try and free it from the pulley.

Meanwhile, the dragon pursed her lips and began to lean her gigantic head in for a kiss. Suddenly the pulley came loose and Shrek fell squarely onto Donkey. Donkey popped out of the dragon's coiled tail, and her kiss landed right on Shrek's rear end.

In his surprise, Shrek let go of the chain, which immediately reeled upward as the candelabra came hurtling down.

Hearing the noise, the dragon reared up in anger—just as the candelabra fell, landing around her neck like a collar. Shrek seized his chance. He grabbed Donkey and ran. The dragon took chase, with the chain unreeling behind her.

Outside the chamber, the princess was still waiting to be rescued. As Shrek went barreling past her, he scooped her up and ran, the dragon blasting fireballs behind them all the way.

Donkey looked at the princess. The princess looked at Donkey.

"Hi, Princess!" said Donkey.

"It talks?" Fiona asked Shrek, pointing to Donkey.

"Yeah," Shrek said with a chuckle. "It's getting him to shut up that's the trick."

"Shrek!" said Donkey, offended.

Shrek was still laughing as they slid down a column and landed with a jarring thump. They ran for the entrance hall of the castle. Shrek started weaving in and out of the pillars, the dragon right behind him. Around and around they went, the chain wrapping itself around one pillar after another as the dragon zigzagged after them.

Shrek stopped and put Fiona and Donkey down. "Okay, you two," he said, "head for the exit. I'll take care of the dragon."

The two of them followed orders and took off, leaving Shrek to face the dragon. It was now or never. With a determined look, Shrek grabbed a sword from the nearby armor of a dead knight. Then, as the chain rocketed past him, he plunged the sword through several of the iron links and deep into the floor. That should hold her for a while.

Shrek ran to join Donkey and Fiona, who were waiting by the exit. "*Ruunnnn!*" he yelled as he rounded the corner.

In front of them lay the bridge. If they could make it across alive, they were home free.

They sprinted as fast as they could onto the rickety bridge. But even though the dragon was pinned in place by her chain, she was not done yet. She was mad.

If there's one thing you don't want behind you as you cross a rickety bridge over a moat of molten lava, it's an angry, fire-breathing dragon. As Shrek and the others made their way onto the bridge, the dragon blasted an extra-large, extra-powerful fireball after them. The fireball ignited the ancient dry wood of the bridge, and as Donkey followed Shrek and Fiona, the flames got closer and closer. Finally there was no bridge left behind him at all, and Donkey could not hang on.

"Aaaaagghhh! Shrek!" he screamed as he began to fall down, down into the boiling lava below.

At the last possible second, Shrek managed to grab Donkey by the tail. The dragon watched helplessly from the castle as they scrambled to the far end of the bridge, just as the last bit of it behind them fell into the inferno below.

Suddenly, the dragon burst through the flames, flying straight at them. They all screamed. But Shrek's plan worked. The chain pulled tight, and the dragon was snapped back and out of sight by the chandelier around her neck. Whew.

Now Shrek, Donkey, and Fiona were dangling by the end of the broken bridge, hanging above the lake of lava. Above them was a sheer cliff. If they couldn't scale it, they'd be cooked. They began to climb the hanging bridge as if it were a rope ladder.

With one last mighty effort, Shrek hauled Fiona over the edge of the cliff. She slid down a small hill and onto safe ground, followed by Donkey. Behind them, they could just make out the figure of the dragon, who was staring mournfully after them, especially Donkey. She let out a defeated cry.

"You did it!" bubbled Fiona as soon as her feet hit the ground. "You rescued me! You're amazing, you're, you're wonderful, you're . . . a little unorthodox, I'll admit," she continued as a very disheveled Shrek dragged his enormous body up over the cliff and tumbled down the hill behind her. "But"—she took a deep breath and regained her poise—"thy deed is great and thine heart is pure," she finished. Then she curtsied prettily. "I am eternally in your debt," she said.

Shrek was not immune to this outpouring of praise. He blushed beneath his helmet, enjoying the attention.

"Ahem," Donkey interrupted, looking just a bit slighted.

Fiona reached down, squeezing Donkey's face indulgently. "And where would a brave knight be without his noble steed?" she said.

"All right!" whooped Donkey. "I hope you heard that, she called me a 'noble steed'! She thinks I'm a steed!" He grinned at the ogre in triumph.

Now Fiona turned to Shrek and giggled. "The battle is won," she said. "You may remove your helmet, good sir knight."

"Ahhh . . . no," said Shrek.

"Why not?"

"I . . . I have helmet hair." Shrek stalled.

"Please," said Fiona coyly. "I would'st look upon the face of my rescuer." She playfully tried to peek under his visor.

Shrek shooed her away. "No, you wouldn'tst."

The princess giggled again. "But—how will you kiss me?" she asked.

Now Shrek traded a bemused look with Donkey. "What?" he said. "That wasn't in the job description."

"Maybe it's a perk," offered Donkey.

"No," said Fiona, "it's destiny. Oh, you must know how it goes: A princess, locked in a tower and beset by a dragon, is rescued by a brave knight, and then they share true love's first kiss."

"*With Shrek?*" hooted Donkey. "You think, wait, whoa, whoa, wait a sec. You think that Shrek is your true love?"

"Well . . . yes," said the princess, somewhat mystified.

"You think Shrek is your true love? Ha, ha, ha!" Donkey howled.

He laughed until he was gasping for air, and just when he was slowing down, he and Shrek exchanged a look, and then both of them burst into a renewed bout of hysterics.

"What is so funny?" Fiona demanded, indignant.

Shrek tried hard to stop laughing. "Let's just say I'm not your type, okay?"

"Of course you are. You're my rescuer!" Fiona was losing patience with all this. "Now, remove your helmet," she commanded.

"Look," Shrek warned her, "I really don't think this is a good idea."

"Just take off the helmet," Fiona repeated.

"I'm not going to."

"Take it off!"

"No!"

Fiona cut him off. "*Now!*" It was clear that she meant business.

"Okay!" said Shrek. "Easy. As ye command, Your Highness." Slowly, he removed his helmet and gave her a shy grin.

Fiona stared at him blankly, confused but not frightened.

"You're . . . an ogre?" said Fiona.

Shrek smiled. "Oh, you were expecting Prince Charming?" he said.

"Well—yes, actually! Oh no! This is all wrong! You're not supposed to be an ogre!"

Shrek sighed. He had heard this sort of thing too often. "Princess, I was sent to rescue you by Lord Farquaad, okay?" he said irritably. "He's the one who wants to marry you."

Fiona looked up at him, surprised. "Well, then why didn't he come rescue me?" she said.

"Good question," Shrek told her. "You should ask him that when we get there."

"But," she sputtered, "I have to be rescued by my true love! Not by some ogre and hi . . . hi . . . his . . . pet!" Tossing her head, she stormed off.

"Well," said Donkey, sounding hurt. "So much for 'noble steed'!"

Shrek glared at Donkey, and then glared toward Fiona. He was going to have to go after her.

"Look, Princess," he said when he'd caught up to her. "You're not making my job any easier."

"Well, I'm sorry, but your job is not my problem. You can tell Lord Farquaad that if he wants to rescue me properly I'll be waiting for him right here." She plonked herself down determinedly on a nearby boulder.

An equally determined look came over Shrek's face. "Hey. I'm no one's messenger boy, okay?" he said. He advanced toward her. "I'm a delivery boy," he said.

"You wouldn't dare!" she screeched as she realized that he was about to pick her up.

But Shrek did dare. He scooped the princess up and flung her over his shoulder into a very inelegant fireman's carry.

"Agghh!" she screamed. "Put me down! Aggghh!"

"You coming, Donkey?" Shrek called casually, over his shoulder.

Donkey jerked to life. "Oh, yep! I'm right behind you," he said.

Fiona was now kicking and screaming. "*Put me down* or you will suffer the consequences! This is not dignified, put me down! Aggghhh!"

twelve
The Princess Worries

ours later, the three of them were still trudging through the forest. Or rather, two of them were trudging. One of them, the princess, was not trudging, because she was still slung over Shrek's shoulder. By this time, she had more or less adjusted to her new position in life. She and Donkey, in fact, had been chatting. Fiona leaned her chin in her hand as she hung over Shrek's back.

"Okay, so here's another question," Donkey was saying. "Say there's a woman that digs you, right, but you don't like her 'that way.' How do you let her down real easy, so her feelings aren't hurt, and you don't get burned to a crisp and eaten? How you do that?"

"Just tell her she's not your true love," Fiona counseled him. She was an expert on this. "Everyone know'st what happens when you find your— oommmppph." She was cut off by a deliberate, bouncing readjustment from Shrek.

"Hey!" she protested. Then she resumed her conversation with Donkey. "The sooner we get to DuLoc the better," she said, annoyed.

"Oh yeah, you're gonna love it there, Princess. It's beautiful," Donkey replied.

Fiona was interested. "And what of my groom-to-be, Lord Farquaad?" she asked him. "What's he like?"

Shrek, noticing a nearby pond, dumped Fiona unceremoniously onto the ground and headed to the pond to wash up. "Well, let me put it this way, Princess," he said, throwing a smile to Donkey. "Men of Farquaad's *stature* are in *short* supply."

Donkey joined in, chuckling. "I dunno, Shrek— there are those who think *little* of him!"

They both broke up as a bewildered Fiona stamped her foot. "Stop it! Stop it, both of you!" she said. "You know, you're just jealous that you could never measure up to a great ruler like Lord Farquaad!" said the princess tartly.

Shrek finished washing up and headed back. "Yeah, well, maybe you're right, Princess," he said, heading back into the trees. "But I'll let you do the measuring when you see him tomorrow."

Fiona stopped cold. "Tomorrow?" she blurted,

suddenly panic-stricken. "It'll take that long?" She looked back fearfully over her shoulder at the setting sun. "Shouldn't we stop to make camp?"

"No," replied Shrek curtly. "That'll take longer." He continued walking. "We can keep going," he said.

"But—it's almost sunset . . ." said Fiona, wild-eyed. "It'll be dark soon."

"That's okay, there'll be a bright moon tonight," said Shrek.

Fiona was growing more agitated by the second, searching for a reason that would convince the ogre to stop. "But . . . there's robbers in the woods," she tried.

Now Donkey was getting worried. "Whoa! Time out," he said. "Shrek, camp is definitely starting to sound good."

Shrek interrupted him in a sarcastic tone of voice. "Hey, come on," he said. "I'm scarier than anything we're gonna see in this forest." He turned and continued walking.

Frustrated beyond words, Fiona jumped in front of Shrek, blocking him. "*I need to find somewhere to camp—now!*" she yelled.

Shrek and Donkey stopped in their tracks and exchanged a glance, a little taken aback.

A few minutes later, Shrek was rolling a large boulder away from the mouth of a cave. "Hey! Over here!" he called to the others.

When they saw Shrek's choice, Donkey was not so

sure. "Shrek," he admonished. "We can do better than that. Now I don't think this is fit for a princess."

But Fiona was more concerned with the approaching sunset than the accommodations. "No, no, it's perfect," she said, a distinct note of urgency in her voice. "It just needs a few homey touches."

Shrek didn't notice her panicky tone. Peering into the cave, he rolled his eyes. "Homey touches? Like what?" he said indignantly.

Suddenly, there was a huge ripping sound that made him pull his head out of the cave and look around. There was Fiona, pulling a tremendous slab of bark off a nearby tree with her bare hands. Shrek and Donkey watched this surprising show of strength in numb amazement.

"A door," said Fiona in reply to his question. She heaved the door over to the cave, looked again at the sun, and faked a quick yawn to cover her hurry. "Well, gentlemen, I bid thee good night," she said, and abruptly pulled the door into place behind her.

Shrek and Donkey look at each other, puzzled. Then Donkey leaned toward the cave door. "Um, you want me to come in there and read you a bedtime story?" he called in. "'Cause I will."

"I said, *good night!*" she called out. Then she slammed the door.

Her two companions looked at each other again. Then Shrek, having heard just about enough from

Fiona, leaned over and made as if to push the boulder back over the mouth of the cave.

Donkey was scandalized. "Shrek, what are you doing?" he said.

"Heh, heh, heh, I just . . . well, you know," he said, trying to cover for what had only sort of been a joke. "Oh, come on, I was just kidding."

Donkey didn't think it was funny, though he had to admit, the princess *was* acting a little strangely.

thirteen
Another One of Those Onion Things

ater that night, Shrek and Donkey lay on their backs around a campfire, gazing at the stars.

". . . and uh, that one," said Shrek, pointing up to a group of stars, "that's Throwback, the only ogre to ever spit over three wheat fields!"

Donkey closed one eye and cocked his head from side to side. Clearly, he wasn't seeing it.

"Right . . . yeah," he said. "Hey, can you tell my future from these stars?"

"Well, the stars don't tell the future, Donkey, they tell stories. Look, there's Bloodnut the Flatulent. You can guess what he's famous for."

"All right, now I know you're making this up!"

"No, look!" Shrek traced the ogre constellation

with his finger, but Donkey just squinted at the stars in confusion. "There he is," Shrek continued, "and there's the group of hunters running away from his stench!"

"Man, that ain't nothin' but a bunch of little dots," said Donkey.

Shrek was starting to get irritated. "You know, Donkey," he said, "sometimes things are more than they appear!" He glanced over to see if Donkey was getting his meaning, but he was greeted by a blank look. "Forget it," said Shrek.

They lay silent for a while, Donkey contemplating the stars and occasionally looking over at Shrek. Finally he sighed. "Hey, Shrek," he said. "What're we gonna do when we get our swamp anyway?"

"*Our* swamp?"

"You know. When we're through rescuing the princess and all that stuff."

"*We?* Donkey, there's no *we*. There's no *our*. There's just me and my swamp. And the first thing I'm gonna do is build a ten-foot wall around my land."

Donkey was taken aback. "You cut me deep, Shrek," he said sadly. "You cut me real deep just now." There was a pause while he gathered himself. "You know what I think?" he said finally. "I think this whole 'wall' thing is just a way to keep somebody out."

Shrek feigned shock. "No!" he said. "D'ya think?"

"Are you hiding something?" probed Donkey.

"Never mind, Donkey," Shrek warned him.

"Ohh. This is another one of those onion things, isn't it?"

"No," Shrek retorted, "this is one of those 'drop it and leave it alone' things!"

"Why don't you want to talk about it?"

"Why do you want to talk about it?"

"*Why are you blocking?*" Donkey demanded.

"I'm not blocking!" roared Shrek.

"Oh yes you are!"

"Donkey! I'm warning you . . ."

"Who are you trying to keep out? Just tell me that, Shrek—who?"

Shrek jumped to his feet. Donkey had really gotten to him this time, really struck a nerve. "Everyone!" he exploded. "Okay?"

At this moment, Donkey wasn't the only one listening. Unseen by either of them, Fiona was peeking around the cave door, eavesdropping on the conversation.

"Oh," Donkey was saying, "now we're gettin' somewhere!"

"Oh, for the love of Pete!" Shrek yelled at him.

The ogre had had enough of this line of conversation. He walked to the edge of the bluff and sat down, staring into the distance, away from Donkey. But Donkey wasn't finished. "Hey, what's your problem, Shrek?" he called over. "What have you got against the whole world anyway, huh?"

"Look, I'm not the one with the problem, okay? It's the world that seems to have a problem with me. People take one look at me and go 'Aaagh! Help! Run! A big, stupid, ugly ogre!'" He sighed. "They judge me before they even know me. That's why I'm better off alone."

Hidden in the shadows of the cave, Fiona's eyes were sympathetic.

Donkey stared silently at Shrek for a moment. Then he walked over to the ogre. The two of them stood silhouetted against the starry sky.

"You know what?" said Donkey. "When we met— I didn't think you were just a big, stupid, ugly ogre."

Shrek glared down at him, but then softened. "Yeah," he grunted. "I know."

A moment went by. Then Donkey smiled and looked up at the stars. "So . . . ah, are there any donkeys up there?" he said.

"Well, there's um, Gabby, the small and annoying," said Shrek, barely able to suppress a smile himself.

Donkey pretended to see it. "Okay, okay, I see it now . . . yeah, the big shiny one, right there, right? That one there?"

"That's the moon."

"Oh . . . oh, okay." Donkey grinned.

At that moment, in Lord Farquaad's bedchamber,

the small yet charming fellow was lying in his big round bed, snuggled in his favorite zebra-print sheets. He was surrounded by his new collection of royal "his and hers" things: towels, gilded coffee mugs, crowns, and everything else his advisers could think of to make him happy, including his and hers wedding outfits for him and Fiona.

"Again, show me again," said Farquaad. "Mirror, mirror. Show her to me. Show me the princess."

The face in the mirror rolled its eyes, but knew better than to argue. So once again, the image of beautiful Fiona in the tower appeared before Farquaad.

"Ahhhh," sighed Lord Farquaad. "She's perfect."

fourteen
Shrek Gets Wounded

The next morning, Fiona was up early. She made her way through the forest, marveling at the nature that surrounded her. Playing the perfect princess, she began to sing. "La, ah, ahhh, la la la laaaa," she trilled.

A small blue bird hopped out of its nest onto a nearby branch and shook off the morning dew. "Cheep, cheep, cheep, *cheeeep!*" it sang in response.

Fiona smiled and waltzed over to it. "La, ah, ahhh, la la la *laaaaa*," she warbled gaily.

The bird twittered back, mirroring her tune again. "Cheep, cheep, cheep, cheep, *cheeeep!*" it went.

Fiona sang a little challenge: "La, la, *laaaaaa.*"

The bird accepted the challenge, going higher: "Cheep, cheep, *cheeeeep.*"

Overjoyed, Fiona sang louder and higher, holding the last horrible note. "La, la, *LAAAAAAAA—*"

The bird trembled, its eyes bulging, and finally started to shake and convulse.

But Fiona, the happy princess, was still holding the note, not even noticing the loud pop, and the little blue feathers that began to drift down through the air.

Finally, one of the feathers drifted past Fiona's nose, startling her. She looked guiltily at the three eggs left in the nest. Oops.

A little later, Shrek awoke to the wonderful smell of eggs frying on a rock skillet. He arose and sniffed happily.

There was Fiona, cooking the eggs over the open fire. Surprised and impressed, Shrek nudged Donkey to show him.

Donkey was dreaming, though. "Ooh, come on, baby," he was saying. "Climb on up in my saddle, and I'll give you a ride—"

"Donkey, wake up!" Shrek whispered loudly.

Donkey sat bolt upright. "Huh? What?" he gasped. Then he saw Shrek. "What?" He yawned.

Shrek pointed to Fiona, and they both stared at her, puzzled.

Finally she noticed that they were awake. "Morning!" she said, a little nervously. "Uhmmm . . . how do you like your eggs?"

"Good mornin', Princess," Donkey greeted her.

"What's all this about?" Shrek wanted to know.

"You know," said Fiona. "We kind of got off to a bad start yesterday and I wanted to make it up to you." She placed the sizzling eggs down in front of Shrek.

"I mean, after all, you did rescue me."

Shrek found himself momentarily speechless. "Ah, thanks," he managed at last.

Fiona brushed her hands on her skirt. "Well, eat up," she said. "We've got a big day ahead of us." Then she went to wash up, leaving Donkey and Shrek looking at each other in wonderment.

In a little while, the three of them were again making their way through the woods toward DuLoc. Shrek licked his fingers, and then let out a loud belch.

"Shrek!" Donkey admonished him.

"What?!" said Shrek. "It's a compliment."

"Well, it's no way to behave in front of a princess," Donkey told him.

Just then, Fiona gave forth with a loud belch of her own. Shrek and Donkey gaped at her, surprised, and in Shrek's case, quite impressed. But Fiona just smiled demurely as she continued walking ahead of them.

"Thanks," she said to Shrek.

Donkey was shocked. "She's as nasty as you are," he said to Shrek.

Shrek laughed. "You know," he said to Fiona, "you're, um, you're not exactly what I expected."

She turned back to him and, with a playful, knowing jab, repeated the words she'd heard him say to Donkey the night before. "Well," she teased, "maybe you shouldn't judge people before you get to know them."

She had that right, Shrek thought to himself as the princess she walked on, humming.

Suddenly, there was a loud swooshing sound and a green blur. Fiona disappeared.

"*La Liberte!*" yelled a voice. Shrek looked up. There was Robin Hood, who had swung in on a vine and snatched the princess.

"Oof!" said Fiona as they landed on a limb above the clearing. "What are you doing?"

"Be still, *mon cheri*," said Robin Hood. "For I am your savior and I am rescuing you from this green . . . beast!" He carpeted Fiona's arm with kisses as she struggled, surprised and indignant.

"Hey! That's my princess!" Shrek yelled. "Go find your own!"

"Ah, please, monster!" said Robin Hood. "Can't you see I'm a little busy?"

Hearing this, Fiona lost it. "Look, pal," she snapped. "I don't know who you think you are, but—"

"Ah, of course," Robin Hood interrupted her. "How rude. Please let me introduce myself." He cupped his hands to his mouth and called into the woods. "Oh, Merry Men!" he gaily sang out.

All at once, the bushes surrounding the clearing began to move. Behind each one was a cleverly camouflaged Merry Man. They were so merry, in fact, that they immediately formed an impromptu chorus line and began to sing.

"Ta da da da da . . . *whooo!*" they went, kicking high as they did the cancan.

"I steal from the rich, and give to the needy," Robin Hood announced, leaping acrobatically down from the tree and landing with a flourish in front of his men, who were now beginning to do their own version of River Dance.

Robin Hood pirouetted in front of the Merry Men as they launched into a musical number with him. "*He takes a wee percentage,*" they sang.

"But I'm not greedy," he added, before singing the next line: "*I rescue pretty damsels. Man, I'm good.*"

"*What a guy!*"

"*Ha-haaah!*" crowed Robin Hood.

"*Monsieur Hood,*" sang the Merry Men.

"Break it down," said Robin Hood as the men went into high dance gear behind him.

"*I like an honest fight and a saucy little maid,*" sang Robin Hood, not noticing that Fiona was getting more and more irate.

"*Pardon our French, but he likes to get—*"

"*Paid,*" sang Robin, finishing the line as the men

rearranged themselves into a large, fancy pattern as they danced.

"*Soooooo*," sang the men.

"*When an ogre in the bush grabs a lady by the tush, that's bad!*" sang Robin.

"*That's bad, that's bad, that's bad!*" echoed the men.

"*When a beauty's with a beast it makes me awfully mad!*"

"*He's mad, he's really mad!*" went the men.

Fiona, still up in the tree, was looking down. Her expression began changing from annoyance to horror as Robin Hood sang the last line: "*Now I'll take my blade and I'll ram it through your heart. Keep your eyes on me, boys, 'cause I'm about to start!*"

The next thing Robin Hood knew, a flying foot had knocked him clean off his feet. The foot belonged to Fiona, who had swung down from the tree to take him out. "Yaaaah!" she hollered. Robin Hood landed against a rock, knocked out cold with a solid crunch, while Fiona did a back flip and landed in front of Shrek.

"Man, that was annoying," she said to the ogre.

The Merry Men weren't quite so merry anymore. "Why, you little . . ." said one of them, taking aim at Fiona with his bow and letting an arrow fly.

Instead of hitting Fiona, though, the arrow whizzed by her and continued on toward Shrek and Donkey, who had leaped into Shrek's arms in fright.

Meanwhile, Little John lunged at Fiona. She adeptly elbowed him in the stomach and then casually back-handed him on the nose.

Next Friar Randy ran at her, determined to bring her down. Coolly, she ran up a tree, back-flipped, and kicked him in the head. Two more men attacked her. She flew into the air, hung suspended and perfectly still for a long, incredible moment—and then scissor-kicked them both at once.

Things continued like this for a while, until, with a series of quick martial-arts moves, Fiona had littered the clearing with unconscious Merry Men.

It was over. Donkey and Shrek looked from Fiona to the men, shocked.

"Shall we?" said Fiona. She looked a little embarrassed as she smoothed out her dress and regained her composure.

They continued on down the road in silence.

Every now and then, Shrek would sneak an admiring glance at Fiona. This princess was full of surprises, that was for sure. This was not your average princess. For starters, this princess had a great left hook.

Finally, he decided to take the bull by the horns. Fiona was walking fast, so he had to hustle to catch up to her. "Whoa. Whoa. Whoa. Whoa, hang on a second," he said. "Wait up. Wait up. Whoa. Where did *that* come from?"

"What?" said Fiona evasively, trying to look innocent.

"That! Back there! That was amazing!"

Fiona just blushed.

"Where'd you learn that?" asked Shrek, impressed.

Fiona tried to look regal. "Oh. Well," she said, "when one lives alone, one has to learn these things in case there's . . ." She stopped short, a surprised look on her face. "There's an arrow in your butt!" she exclaimed.

Shrek was confused. "What?" he said.

Fiona pointed downward. There was a small arrow, jutting out of Shrek's enormous behind. "Oh, would you look at that," he said, twisting to inspect it.

"Oh no! This is all my fault. I'm so sorry!" cried Fiona.

As Shrek tried to pull out arrow, Donkey caught up with them. "What's wrong?" he asked anxiously.

"Shrek's hurt," said Fiona.

That was all Donkey needed to hear. Now he was frantic. He began to scamper around hysterically, generally getting in the way.

"Shrek's hurt? Shrek's hurt? Oh no! Shrek's gonna die," he wailed.

"*Donkey.* I'm okay," Shrek assured him.

But Donkey just kept dithering. "Oh, you can't do this to me, Shrek! I'm too young for you to die! Keep your legs elevated. Turn your head and cough. Does anyone know the Heimlich?"

Finally Fiona grabbed the donkey's head, pulling it around toward her. "Donkey! Calm down!" she barked at him. "If you want to help Shrek, run into the woods and find me a blue flower with red thorns."

This snapped Donkey out of his panic. He had an important job to do. "Blue flower, red thorns," he repeated. "Okay. I'm on it. Blue flower, red thorns. Blue flower, red thorns. Don't die, Shrek," he pleaded as he headed for the woods. "And if you see a long tunnel, *stay away from the light!*"

"Donkey!" yelled Fiona and Shrek together.

"Oh, yeah right," said Donkey, snapping out of it once again. He marched into the trees. "Blue flower, red thorns. Blue flower, red thorns . . ." he chanted.

"What are the flowers for?" Shrek asked Fiona when he was gone.

"For getting rid of Donkey," she replied.

"Ah!" he said, getting it.

"Now," she said, inspecting the arrow. "You hold still and I'll yank this thing out." She grabbed hold of it and began to pull.

"Ow!" Shrek yelped. "Hey! Easy with the yankin'."

"Well, I'm sorry, but it, but it has to come out . . . Now, now lemme . . . Now hold on . . . don't move. . . ."

"No, it's tender. Hey, would ya . . . What you're doing is the opposite of help."

Fiona kept wiggling the arrow, and Shrek kept pulling away from her. Finally he grabbed her whole face with one hand and held it there. "Okay. Look. Look. Time out," he said.

"Would you . . ." she began, annoyed. "Okay. What do you propose we do?" she asked him.

Deep in the woods, Donkey was frantically searching through the underbrush. "Blue flower, red thorns," he muttered to himself. "Blue flower, red thorns. Blue flower, red thorns. This would be so much easier if I wasn't color blind!"

Suddenly he heard a yell from Shrek. "Owww!" it went.

Quickly pinching off the nearest bunch of blossoms with his teeth, he began flailing his way back toward the clearing. "Hold on, Shrek, I'm coming!" he yelled, in a voice muffled by a mouthful of flowers.

In the clearing, Shrek and Fiona were arguing over the delicate medical procedure in progress. Shrek lay on the ground, facedown, while Fiona stood over him, using both hands as she tried mightily to wrench the arrow from Shrek's rear end.

"Ow!" Shrek yelled again. "Not good!"

"Okay. N—okay. I can nearly see the head. . . . It's just about there."

Shrek had had enough. All this wiggling and pulling was really starting to hurt! He rolled over. As he did, he knocked Fiona off her feet, causing her to land directly on top of him.

Donkey raced into the clearing, screeching to a halt when he saw them.

"Ahem," said Donkey politely.

Startled, Shrek pushed Fiona off him and rolled over to face Donkey. "Nothing happened," he explained hastily. "We just . . . ah . . ."

"Look," said Donkey, "if you two wanted to be alone, all you had to do was ask, okay?"

"Oh, come on," said Shrek. "Believe me. That's the last thing on my mind. The princess here was just helpin' me get this . . ."

In one great pull, Fiona quickly ripped the arrow out of Shrek's butt.

"Ow!" cried the ogre. "Ow."

Donkey took one look at the arrow in the princess's hand and went pale. "Hey, what's that? Hee, hee, hee," he gibbered. "That's—Is that blood?" He then fainted dead away.

Without a word, Shrek picked him up and threw him over his shoulder. The three of them continued down the road.

fifteen
Fiona's Secret

he journey toward DuLoc continued. But something was different. Whatever tension had existed between Shrek and Fiona before was now gone.

When they came to a river where there was no bridge, Shrek grabbed a tree and easily bent it over to make a bridge for the others. But, lost in Fiona's eyes, he let the tree go before Donkey managed to make it across, flinging Donkey off. Shrek and Fiona didn't even notice.

They kept walking, Donkey trailing behind. To help pass the time, Shrek caught a frog and inflated it, making a lovely balloon for Fiona. Fiona returned the favor with her own creation, a balloon doggie made from an inflated snake. She found a big sticky spiderweb full of trapped flies, and spun it on a stick until it resembled a big wad of cotton candy for Shrek. They playfully shoved each other as they walked side by side.

After a while, they broke out of the woods onto a small rise where an old, ruined mill was perched. The neat fields of DuLoc stretched out before them, and in the distance, the castle stood out like a big eyesore.

"There it is," said Shrek. "Your future awaits you."

"That's DuLoc?" she asked wistfully.

Shrek looked at her hesitantly, but she didn't move. "Well, um . . ." he said at last, "I, uh . . . I guess we better move on."

"Sure, but Shrek?" she said, keeping one eye on the setting sun, "I'm . . . I'm worried about Donkey."

"What?" he said.

"I mean, look at him. He, he doesn't look so good." She looked up at Shrek. Shrek looked at her. "Does he?" she added for emphasis.

"What are you talking about? I'm fine," Donkey protested.

"Well," said Fiona, "that's what they always say, and then . . . then, next thing you know, you're on your back. Dead."

Shrek was finally understanding where Fiona was going with this. Did they have to rush to DuLoc so fast? "You know, she's right," he told Donkey, stalling for time. "You look awful. Do you want to sit down?"

"Well, you know, I'll make you some tea," Fiona chimed in.

They both looked intently at Donkey, who was starting to get intimidated. "Well, I didn't wanna say anything," he said, "but I got this twinge in my neck, when I turn my head like this. Look." He turned his head. "Ow. See?"

"Who's hungry?" said Shrek instantly. "I'll find us some dinner."

"I'll get the firewood," Fiona offered quickly.

Fiona and Shrek darted off in opposite directions, leaving the confused Donkey looking back and forth after them. "Hey, where you going? Oh, man, I can't feel my toes. I don't have any toes! I think I need a hug," he added mournfully.

Soon Fiona and Shrek were sitting beside an open fire, Donkey a little distance away. Shrek was cooking something on a spit.

"Mmm. This is good," said Fiona, taking another bite. "This is *really* good! What is this?"

"Weedrat," Shrek replied. "Rotisserie-style."

Fiona took another bite. "No kidding? Well, this is delicious."

"Well, they're also great in stews," said Shrek enthusiastically. It wasn't often that someone appreciated his cooking. Never, in fact. "Now I don't mean to brag, but I make a mean weedrat stew."

Fiona smiled, but her smile quickly faded. She sighed. "I guess I'll be dining a little differently tomorrow night," she said. In the distance she could see Farquaad's castle, where she was to be wed the next day.

"Maybe you can come visit me in the swamp sometime," Shrek offered. "I'll cook all kinds of stuff for you—swamp toad soup, fish-eye tartare. You name it."

Fiona took a long look at Shrek, smiling. "Hmm," she said. "I'd like that."

They locked eyes for a long moment. Then Shrek slurped a rat tail into his mouth. "Um, Princess . . . ?" he said with a nervous laugh. He looked as if he was considering telling her something serious.

She gave him a significant look. "Yes . . . Shrek?"

"I, um, I was wondering," he began. "Are you . . ." He chickened out. "Are you gonna eat that?" he finished.

Fiona grinned and handed her barbecued weedrat to Shrek. Their hands lingered briefly as they both held on to it.

At this moment, Donkey came up beside them. "Man—isn't this romantic!" he enthused.

"Just look at that sunset."

Shrek and Fiona looked up, startled out of their moment. Instantly, Fiona's mood changed. She sat up abruptly and spun around to face the sunset.

"Sunset!" she cried. "Oh no! I mean—it's late. It's

very late." She leaped to her feet, a desperate look on her face.

"What?" said Shrek.

Fiona was helpless to explain. "Well, I . . . I . . . I just . . ." she floundered.

"Wait a minute," Donkey interrupted. "I see what's going on here."

Fiona looked at him, frozen with panic.

"You're afraid of the dark, aren't you?" he said triumphantly.

A huge sigh of relief escaped Fiona. "Uhhh . . . yes! Yes, that's it! I'm terrified. I . . . You know what? I better go inside." She backed up toward the mill.

"Well, don't feel bad, Princess," Donkey reassured her. "I used to be afraid of the dark too, until—Hey, no, wait, I'm still afraid of the dark. It's spinach I'm not afraid of."

With a sad smile, Fiona headed up the mill house steps. "Good night," she said to them. Then she looked down one last time and went into the mill, closing the door behind her.

"Good night," said Shrek, mystified.

Donkey looked back and forth between the door and Shrek. "Oh, now I really see what's going on here," he said.

Shrek finally tore his eyes away from the mill door. "What're you talking about?" he asked Donkey.

Donkey trotted over to the fire. "Hey, I don't even

want to hear it," he said. "Look. I'm an animal, and I got instincts, and I know that you two were digging on each other. I could feel it."

"Oh, you're crazy. I'm just bringing her back to Farquaad."

"Oh, c'mon, Shrek, wake up! Just go on in and tell her how you feel."

"I . . . There's nothing to tell," snapped Shrek. Then he sighed resignedly. "Besides, even if I did tell her that—well, you know—and I'm not saying I do, 'cause I don't. She's a princess and I'm . . ."

"An ogre?"

"Yeah. An ogre." Shrek turned and headed into the woods.

"Hey. Where're you goin'?" Donkey called after him.

"To get more firewood."

Donkey looked over at the fire and noticed a huge pile of wood that was still unburned. Shrek wasn't going off to get any firewood. He just wanted to be alone.

Shrek, meanwhile, had stumbled upon a field of sunflowers that overlooked DuLoc. As he sat and gazed at the town in the growing darkness, an idea crossed his face.

A little while later, Donkey was entering the abandoned mill. It was a spooky place, filled with shadows and fallen beams lying at crazy angles.

Donkey picked his way through the gloom with a sense of foreboding.

"Princess?" he whispered. "Princess Fiona? Princess, where are you? Princess, it's very spooky in here, I'm not playing games, now . . ."

He heard a clang, then nothing. He was growing more uneasy by the second.

Suddenly, a rotted beam broke in half above him with a resounding crack. *Whump!* Something fell down from above, landing very close to Donkey.

"Ahhhhh!" screamed Donkey.

"Ahhhh!" screamed . . . whatever it was.

In the murky darkness, Donkey could just barely make out the figure that was picking itself up from the floor. It was big. It was scary. It was some kind of a monster.

"Noooooo!" it cried, in a voice that was somehow oddly familiar to Donkey. "No!"

Donkey panicked, looking for a way out, but he was cornered. The lines of the figure were becoming clearer as his eyes got more accustomed to the darkness. It was some kind of an ogress. "Oh no! Help!" shrieked Donkey.

"Shhhhhh!" said the ogress.

"Shrek! Shrek! Shrek!" Donkey hollered.

"No! No! It's okay! It's okay!" the ogress whispered furiously.

"What'd you do with the princess?" Donkey demanded of her.

Now the ogress emerged from the shadows. "Donkey. Shhhhh! I'm the princess. It's me. In this body," she whispered.

"Oh my god. You ate the princess!" He leaned down and pressed his ear to the ogress's stomach. "Can you hear me?" he yelled into her middle. "Listen, keep breathing!"

"Donkey!" said the ogress, exasperated.

Donkey was still talking to her stomach. "I'll get you out of there!" he called. Then he headed for the door, yelling for help again. "Shrek! Shrek!"

The ogress clapped her hand over Donkey's mouth, trying to calm him. "Shhhh! This is me!" she said gently, trying to calm him down.

"Mmm*rek*!" said Donkey, his voice muffled by the huge hand. He struggled, wild-eyed, against his captor.

And then, all at once, his eyes met hers—and there in her eyes he saw Fiona. He stopped yelling and she gently took her hand off his mouth.

"Princess . . . ? What happened to you? You're uh . . . uh . . . different." For once, he was at a loss for words.

Fiona turned away from him, fighting back tears. "I'm ugly, okay?" she said bitterly.

"Well, yeah. Well, was it something that you ate? 'Cause I told Shrek those rats were a bad idea! 'You are what you eat,' I said."

"No!" she interrupted him, at the end of her rope. Then she turned away from him and sighed. "I've been this way as long as I remember," she told him.

"What do you mean? Look, I've never seen you like this before."

"It only happens when the sun goes down." Fiona leaned over a barrel of water, looking down at her reflection. She was caught up in her own thoughts. "'By night one way, by day another,'" she said. "'This shall be the norm. Until you find true love's first kiss. And then take love's true form.'"

"Ahh . . . that's beautiful. I didn't know you wrote poetry."

"It's a spell," she corrected him. "When I was a little girl a witch cast a spell on me. Every night I become this"—she gazed down into her reflection again and then splashed the water with her hand, dashing the image to bits—"this horrible, ugly beast!" she finished, strangling a sob.

She turned back to Donkey and continued in a choked voice. "I was placed in a tower to await the day my true love would rescue me. That's why I have to marry Lord Farquaad tomorrow. Before the sun sets and he sees me . . . like this." Slumping to the floor, she held her head and wept.

Donkey wasn't quite sure what to say, but did his best to console her. "All right, all right, calm down. Look, it's not that bad. You're not that ugly. Well, okay, I'm not gonna lie—you are ugly. But you only look like this at night. Shrek's ugly twenty-four seven."

"But, Donkey, I'm a *princess*—and this is not how a princess is meant to look."

This only made Fiona cry harder.

"Princess? How 'bout if you don't marry Lord Farquaad?"

"I have to!" she cried. "Only my true love's kiss can break the spell."

"But, you know . . . you're kind of an ogre, and Shrek's . . . well, you've got a lot in common," Donkey told her.

"Shrek?"

sixteen
From Bad to Worse

t that moment, Shrek was approaching the mill house, a wide smile on his face. He was holding a sunflower.

"Princess," Shrek said, rehearsing his speech, "I—How's it going, first of all? Good, um, good for me, too. I'm okay. I saw this flower and thought of you 'cause it's pretty and, well, I don't really like it, but I thought you'd like it 'cause you're pretty—but I like you anyway. . . . Oh, I'm in trouble," he trailed off with a groan. He took a deep breath as he climbed the steps. "Okay, here we go," he told himself.

When he reached the door, he put his hand up to knock. But what was this? Voices? Who could be in there with the princess? His hand hovered an inch from the door.

Shrek opened the door a crack.

". . . who could ever love a beast so hideous and ugly?" Fiona was saying. "Princess and ugly don't go together. That's why I can't stay here with Shrek. My only chance to live happily ever after is to marry my true love."

Shrek's face looked numb with shock as he closed the door. He thought she liked him! How could he have been such an idiot?

"Don't you see, Donkey?" Shrek heard as he turned away from the door. "That's just how it has to be."

Fiona's words echoed through Shrek's head. "Princess and ugly don't go together." Crushed by this thought, he dropped the sunflower and moved off, a ruined hulk.

Up in the mill house, Fiona was still talking, totally unaware that Shrek had been outside the door. "It's the only way to break the spell," she said to Donkey.

"Well, you gotta tell Shrek the truth," Donkey replied.

"No! No. You can't breathe a word. No one must ever know!"

Donkey could hardly stand it. "What's the point of being able to talk if you gotta keep secrets!" he complained.

"Promise you won't tell. Promise!"

"All right, all right. I won't tell him," he promised. "But you should."

It was time for Donkey to go. As he walked down the steps, he muttered to himself, "I just know that before this is over I'm gonna need a whole lot of serious therapy. Look at my eye twitching."

Fiona watched him leave. But as she looked down through the open door she saw something on the ground. She reached down and picked up the sunflower Shrek had left behind.

Later that night, as Donkey slept out by the fire, the ogress that Fiona was lay awake. She held the sunflower, picking the petals off one by one, mulling something over. "I tell him. I tell him not. I tell him, I tell him not," she chanted to herself.

She picked off the last petal. Dissatisfied, she plucked the whole head off the stem. "I tell him," she said with conviction.

She got up and headed out the door in her full hideous form. "Shrek!" she called out. "Shrek! There's something I want . . ."

But Shrek was not by the fire. In fact, he was nowhere to be seen. Fiona looked around for him, not noticing that the sun was rising above the horizon.

As its first ray hit Fiona, there was a blinding flare of white, and she was transformed back into her daytime self.

Now, against the morning light, she saw a lone figure approaching. It was Shrek. She smiled, the beautiful sunshine streaming over her and Shrek. He almost looked like a knight in shining armor. It was a misty, magic moment. She ran to greet him, full of happiness.

But as Shrek got closer, his face became visible against the sun—and he looked mighty mad. Fiona stopped in her tracks.

"Shrek! Are you all right?" she said.

"Perfect. Never been better." There was a nasty tone to his voice. He walked right past her, forcing her to trot to keep up.

"I . . . I don't . . . There's something I have to tell you," she said.

"You don't have to tell me anything, Princess. I heard enough last night."

"You heard what I said?"

"Every word," said Shrek.

"I thought you'd understand," she said, stung by his callous tone.

"Oh, I understand. Like you said: 'Who could love a hideous ugly beast?'"

The princess was devastated. If there was anybody who could overlook her . . . problem, she thought, it would have been Shrek. "But . . . I thought that wouldn't matter to you," she mumbled, half to herself.

"Oh, yeah?" Shrek replied. "Well it does."

It was no use. Shrek couldn't know that he hadn't heard everything she'd said, and neither could Fiona.

So there he was, thinking she'd been calling him a hideous, ugly beast. And there she was, assuming he'd understood she'd been talking about herself.

This impossible discussion was about over anyway, but it was suddenly interrupted by a sound. It was a sort of rumbling, clanking noise: the sound of a lot of soldiers on horseback. It was Farquaad's approaching army. A fanfare announced his impending arrival.

"Ah, right on time," said Shrek sarcastically. "Princess, I've brought you a little something."

Fiona listened in horror to the rapidly approaching sound. In a minute, the army was upon them, Farquaad at the forefront.

Donkey, sleeping by the smoldering fire, jumped up with a start. "What'd I miss? What'd I miss?" he said, still half-asleep. But then, seeing the soldiers looming above him, he shrank back. "Who said that?" he muttered, trying not to move his lips. "Couldn't have been the donkey."

Farquaad pulled his horse up in front of Shrek and Fiona. He was dressed in his most resplendent knight-in-shining-armor outfit, and it glinted in the sunlight. "Princess Fiona?" he said, eyeing her up and down.

The princess was too stunned to reply. This was all happening way, way too fast.

In the silence, Shrek stepped forward. "As promised," he said to Farquaad. "Now, hand it over."

Farquaad held a large, official-looking piece of

parchment to Shrek. "Very well, ogre," he said flippantly. "The deed to your swamp. Cleared out as agreed. Take it and go, before I change my mind."

Fiona looked at Shrek. Shrek looked at Fiona. Then Shrek snatched the deed out of Farquaad's hand and turned his back abruptly, not looking at the look of horror on Fiona's face as she realized for the first time that she was being traded like a piece of property.

From high on his mighty steed, Lord Farquaad spoke to Fiona. "Forgive me, Princess, for startling you," he said. "But you startled *me*—for I have never seen such a radiant beauty before. I am Lord Farquaad."

Fiona worked to compose herself. "Lord Farquaad. Oh no. No. Forgive me, my lord, for I was just saying a short . . ."

As if the word had been his cue, Farquaad snapped his fingers, and a guard lifted him off his mount. Left behind on the horse was the pair of leg extenders that had reached down to the stirrups and made him look so tall in the saddle. He now stood on the ground, all four and a half squatty feet of him.

". . . farewell," Fiona concluded, trying not to stare at her new suitor.

Farquaad didn't notice. "Oh, that is so sweet." He chuckled. "You don't have to waste good manners on the ogre. It's not like it has feelings."

Fiona looked at Shrek, who was still walking away.

Her face turned hard. "No, you're right," she said. "'*It*' doesn't."

With some difficulty, Farquaad got down on his knee before Fiona and took her hand. This had the effect of pulling her down sharply.

"Princess Fiona," he began, "beautiful, fair, flawless Fiona . . . I ask your hand in marriage. Will you be the perfect bride for the perfect groom?"

Fiona was still watching Shrek. "Lord Farquaad," she said, glaring at the ogre's back, "I accept. Nothing would make me happier." She made sure to speak loudly enough that Shrek would hear every word. If he didn't care about her, she certainly wasn't going to make a fool of herself for him.

"Excellent!" said Farquaad. "I'll start the plans . . . for tomorrow we wed!"

"No!" Fiona blurted out.

Hearing this, Shrek spun around, a hopeful look on his face.

But the thing had been set in motion, and Fiona was too hurt to stop it. She still just wanted to wound Shrek. "I mean—ah, why wait?" she said, trying to cover her outburst. "Let's get married today. Before sunset."

Shrek's moment of hope had disappeared. He scowled and turned away.

"Oh! Anxious, are we?" Farquaad said to Fiona, quite pleased that she seemed so smitten with him.

"You're right. The sooner the better. There's so much to do!"

He snapped his fingers again, and the guards lifted him back onto his saddle and into the extend-o-legs. When he was firmly settled up there, looking regal again, one of the guards bent to help Fiona up. But before he could lift her, she hopped onto the horse on her own, arranging herself so she was sitting sidesaddle behind Farquaad. It made the perfect, storybook image—the rescue of the beautiful maiden in distress.

Watching all this, Donkey looked desperately back and forth between Shrek and Fiona as they parted ways. How could this be happening? Why didn't either of them come to their senses? Shrek and Fiona were meant to be! Anybody could see it. Even him!

In a panic, he chased after Shrek, just as the departing royal party was sweeping past the ogre. Farquaad was already counting on his fingers. "There's the caterer, the cake, the band, the guest list. Captain," he ordered, "round up some guests!"

Fiona flung one last spiteful look at Shrek. "Fare thee well, ogre," she said bitterly.

Shrek frowned as they rode off, and then turned to stomp out the fire. Donkey caught up to him, breathless.

"Shrek!" he gasped. "What are you doing? You're letting her get away!"

"Yeah, so what?"

The fire now dead, Shrek struck off in the direction of his swamp. Donkey tried to keep up, still looking back and forth from Shrek to the disappearing soldiers. "Shrek," he said, "there's something about her that you don't know. Look, I—I talked to her last night. She's—"

Shrek wheeled on Donkey. "Yeah, I know you talked to her last night. You're great pals aren't you? Now, if you two are such good friends, why don't you follow *her* home?"

"But Shrek, I want to go with you."

"Hey, I told you, didn't I? You're not coming home with me," Shrek snarled. "I live alone! My swamp, me. Nobody else, understand? Nobody! Especially useless, pathetic, annoying, *talking* donkeys!"

"But—I thought—"

"Yeah, well, you know what? You thought wrong!" He stalked off, walking fast, and disappeared over the hill.

And so, the story seemed to have ended, and not happily. Shrek, Fiona, Farquaad, and Donkey went their separate ways—Shrek back to his cleared-out swamp, Fiona and Farquaad to DuLoc, and Donkey to wander the land alone.

In the castle, Fiona and Farquaad prepared for the wedding. Farquaad bustled about, brimming with good cheer, polishing his crown, seeing to all the details.

But Fiona looked very, very sad. She had made her decision, but it did not make her happy. When the extravagant wedding cake was delivered, she stood and stared dejectedly at it. Standing on top were a little bride and groom. She reached out and pressed the groom halfway down into the cake, so that it barely came up to the bride's shoulder. There. That was more like the way it was.

At the same time, Shrek was busy cleaning all the fairy-tale debris from his swamp. He swept up fairy dust, threw magic wands into the trash, picked up forgotten leprechaun hats. At last, he had the place to himself again. He wore the face of someone trying to convince himself that he was happy.

In her room in the castle, Fiona tried on her wedding veil. There was a faraway look in her eyes.

And Donkey? He was out in the world on his own—until, who should he bump into but his old friend the dragon. He came upon her sitting by the river, looking sad and lonesome. She'd been looking for him. She missed him. Feeling guilty, he sat down beside her, and they had a long, long talk.

seventeen
Go Ask Fiona

That afternoon, Shrek was just settling down to a solitary meal of worms in leech sauce. But his heart really wasn't in it; for once, he had no appetite. He pushed the dish away.

Then he heard a noise outside his hut. Farquaad had gotten rid of all his uninvited guests. So who could be making that infernal racket outside? He got up and went out to see what it was.

And there was Donkey, right in the front yard. He was assembling a line of small rocks and branches.

"Donkey? What are you doing?" Shrek inquired.

"I would think you of all people would recognize a wall when you see one!" replied Donkey, still working.

Shrek squinted at it. "Well—yeah. But the wall's supposed to go around my swamp, not through it."

"It is. Around *your* half. See? That's your half, and this is my half." Donkey gestured this way and that.

"Oh—your half?" said Shrek. "Hmmm."

"Yes, my half. I helped rescue the princess. I did half the work. I get half the booty. Now hand me that big ol' rock, the one that looks like your head."

Shrek was not amused. "Back off," he warned.

"No, *you* back off."

Shrek started to pull down the wall as Donkey continued to build it. Picking up a branch, he started to throw it down, but Donkey blocked his way. They began to struggle over the branch, and the fight built in pitch.

"This is my swamp!" roared Shrek.

"Our swamp!" retorted Donkey.

"Let go, Donkey!" Shrek grunted.

"*You* let go!" yelled Donkey.

"Stubborn jackass!"

"Smelly ogre!"

Without another word, Shrek suddenly let go of the branch, sending Donkey tumbling backward. "Fine!" he shouted, storming off toward his house.

"Hey! Hey, come back here!" Donkey called after him. "I'm not through with you yet."

"Well, *I'm* through with *you!*"

Now Donkey ran in front of Shrek, blocking his

way. Shrek turned and walked in another direction, trying to get around him. This happened over and over, with Donkey blocking his way each time, until they ended up in front of the outhouse. The whole time, Donkey continued his tirade.

"Uh-uh!" he ranted. "You know, with you it's always me, me, me. Well, guess what? Now it's my turn, so you just shut up and pay attention. You are mean to me, you insult me, and you don't appreciate anything that I do. You're always pushing me around or pushing me away!"

"Oh yeah? Well, if I treated you so bad, how come you came back?"

"Because that's what friends do!" cried Donkey. "They forgive each other!"

There was a brief silence. "Oh yeah," Shrek said, sounding almost apologetic. "Yeah, you're right, Donkey." Then his face hardened, and he gave Donkey a bitter look. "I forgive you," he said, "for stabbing me in the back!" Then he spun and stormed into his outhouse, slamming the door behind him.

Donkey was so exasperated he could hardly find the words to talk. "Uhhhhh!" he screeched. "You're so wrapped up in layers, onion boy, you're afraid of your own feelings."

"Go away!" yelled Shrek from behind the outhouse door.

"See! There you are, doing it again. Just like you

did to Fiona. And all she ever did was like you. Maybe even love you."

"Love me? She said I was ugly! A hideous creature! I heard the two of you talking."

"She wasn't talking about you!" Donkey yelled through the door. "She was talking about . . ." Suddenly he remembered his promise to Fiona. "Uh . . . somebody else," he finished up lamely.

There was a lengthy silence. Then Shrek slowly opened the door. "She wasn't talking about me?" he said. "Well, then, who was she talking about?"

"Uh-uh. No way. I'm not saying anything."

"Donkey!" Shrek bellowed in frustration.

Donkey held his ground, defiant now, and silent for the first time. He gave Shrek a pointed look.

"Okay—look, I'm sorry, all right?" It was very, very hard for Shrek to apologize, and he did it grudgingly.

Donkey kind of liked this new development. But he wanted a *real* apology. He raised an eyebrow.

"I'm sorry," Shrek repeated. "I guess I am just a big, stupid . . . ugly ogre!" He paused, his feelings in visible turmoil. "Can you forgive me?" he said at last.

Donkey looked Shrek up and down and decided that the ogre was being sincere. "Hey, that's what friends are for, right?"

Shrek smiled. "Right. Friends?"

"Friends," agreed Donkey. They shook on it.

There was an uncomfortable pause, since neither of them knew quite what to say next. Finally, Shrek broke the silence. "So, um, what *did* Fiona say about me?" he asked.

"What are you asking me for? Why don't you just go ask her?"

A look of resolute determination crossed Shrek's face. He would. He'd do it. He'd go ask Fiona.

Then, suddenly, he jumped about a foot. "Oh no!" he cried. "The wedding! We'll never make it in time!"

Donkey laughed a dashing, debonair laugh. "Ha ha. Never fear," he said. "For where there's a will, there's a way—and I have a way!"

Donkey whistled loudly. In seconds, there was a huge whirring sound, and Shrek looked up to see the dragon, hovering overhead like a rescue copter.

"Donkey?!" said Shrek in amazement.

Donkey laughed. "I guess it's just my animal magnetism," he said.

Shrek laughed, too, a booming laugh that shook the treetops. "Ha, ha, ha. Aww, come here, you." Then he bent down and, grabbing Donkey around the neck, gave him a playful noogie—the closest he could get to a hug.

"All right, all right," said Donkey, "don't get all slobbery. No one likes a kiss-up."

The dragon dropped the chain that was still slung around her neck, and the two friends climbed up.

"All right, hop on!" said Donkey. "And hold on tight. I haven't had a chance to install my seat belts yet."

And so, holding on for dear life, they flew through the clouds over the green land, on a direct path to DuLoc.

eighteen
The Ogre Objects

t the cathedral in DuLoc, the ceremony was already in progress. It was everything a royal marriage of convenience ought to be. Hundreds of DuLocians watched with reverence and awe, thanks to the guards who held signs reading REVERENCE and AWE. Thelonious stood nearby, holding a velvet pillow on which rested the two rings. The bishop had already begun the vows.

"People of DuLoc," he intoned, "we gather here today to bear witness to the union of our new king and queen."

Fiona glanced nervously at the window, where the sun was slowly dropping toward the horizon. "Excuse me," she politely interrupted the bishop, "um . . . could we just skip to the 'I dos'?"

Farquaad chuckled indulgently at his bride's eagerness. "Ha, ha, ha. Go on," he said, grinning and motioning for the bishop to speed things up.

Suddenly, outside the cathedral, the dragon dropped like a stone from the sky, shaking the ground as she landed. The guards immediately fled in terror.

The dragon looked quizzically at Shrek and Donkey on her back.

"Go ahead, have some fun," Donkey told her. "If we need you, I'll whistle. How about that?"

Shrek and Donkey climbed down and the dragon took off, looking thrilled at the prospects for mayhem that awaited her in the town.

Shrek headed for the cathedral door, but Donkey stopped him before he got there.

"Hey, Shrek," he said. "Wait a minute. Look, you wanna do this right, don't you?"

"What are you talking about?"

"There's a line, a line you gotta wait for," Donkey explained. "The priest is gonna say, 'Speak now or forever hold your peace,' and that's when you say, 'I object!'"

"Oh, I don't have time for this!" said Shrek. He pushed past Donkey and reached for the door handle.

"Hey, wait! Wait! What are you doing? Listen to me!"

Shrek listened, impatient.

"Look, you love this woman, don't you?" Donkey continued.

"Yes," said Shrek hesitantly.

"Then you gotta try a little tenderness! The chicks love that romantic stuff."

"All right! All right! When does this guy say the line?"

"We gotta check it out!"

A moment later, if anybody inside had been looking toward the rear of the sanctuary, they would have seen Donkey's head popping up outside the high window. Then he dropped away. He reappeared, then dropped out of sight again.

Outside, Shrek was hefting Donkey up and catching him over and over. "What do you see?" he asked Donkey.

"They're at the altar," said Donkey as he fell.

Once again, Donkey popped up into the window.

". . . and by the power vested in me," the bishop was saying, "I now pronounce you husband and wife, king and queen . . ."

"Holy dragon-breath! He already said it!" cried Donkey, still airborne in front of the window.

"Oh, for the love of Pete," said Shrek.

So much for Donkey's big plan. Shrek leaped for the door and burst into the cathedral.

"I *object*!" he thundered.

Farquaad, about to kiss Fiona, turned to see what the interruption was. Fiona turned, too. When she saw Shrek, her jaw dropped in shock.

A gasp went through the rear pews, and rolled forward as Shrek made his way toward the altar. People recoiled from the ogre as Shrek strode determinedly forward.

"Shrek . . . ?" said Fiona, in a hopeful, wistful sort of voice.

"Oh, now what does it want?" said Farquaad peevishly.

Shrek continued making his way to the front of the cathedral. "Hi, everyone!" he said, keeping his voice jolly in order to reassure the crowd. "Having a good time, are you? I love DuLoc, first of all—very clean."

Fiona glanced toward the setting sun. Then she turned to Shrek, a little angry and desperate, cutting him off. "What are you doing here?" she demanded. The sun was about to go down, and if she hadn't kissed Farquaad yet there would be big, big trouble.

"Really," Farquaad told Shrek, "it's rude enough being alive when no one wants you, but showing up uninvited to a wedding . . ."

Shrek ignored him. "Fiona—I need to talk to you," he said.

"Oh?" she returned angrily. "Now you want to talk? Well, it's a little late for that. So if you'll excuse me . . ."

She turned back to Farquaad, ready for the ceremonial kiss. Farquaad puckered up.

But Shrek grabbed her arm, spinning her to face him. "You can't marry him!" he said.

"And why not?" spat Fiona accusingly.

"Because—because he's just marrying you so he can be king."

"Outrageous!" said Farquaad indignantly. "Fiona, don't listen—"

"He's not your true love," Shrek persisted.

"What do you know about true love?" Fiona demanded.

Farquaad started laughing, motioning to the sign-bearer to hold up a sign reading "Laugh."

"Oh, this is precious!" Farquaad giggled. "The ogre has fallen in love with the princess. Oh, good Lord. Ha. Ha. Ha. An ogre and a princess?"

The audience laughed. But Fiona was not laughing. She stepped toward Shrek, staring at him. "Shrek? Is this true?" she said softly.

Farquaad saw that he was losing the moment. "Who cares! It's preposterous!" he announced, stepping forward to grab Fiona's arm. "Fiona, my love, we're but a kiss away from our happily ever after. Now kiss me."

Farquaad puckered up again, ready to kiss her. But she just looked at him warily.

The sun was setting.

Fiona looked to Shrek, and then back at Farquaad,

whose eyes were closed and lips still puckered. Then she backed away from Farquaad.

She looked right at Shrek. "*By night one way, by day another,*" she said. "I wanted to show you before . . ."

Without finishing the sentence, Fiona closed her eyes and waited. The sun dropped below the horizon. And as the light faded, Fiona began to transform. She grew taller and wider, her skin turned green to match Shrek's, her nose got lumpy, her ears changed shape.

Farquaad's eyes were now open, and they grew wide with shock and revulsion as he stared at the ogress Fiona. The crowd gasped in horror. Someone passed out.

And Shrek? He stared at Fiona in astonishment as her form changed. Then he grinned. "Well," he said. "That explains a lot!"

Fiona locked eyes with Shrek. She smiled in pleasant surprise.

Farquaad was backing away, horrified at the sight of the Fiona ogress. "Ewww!" he said. "It's disgusting! Guards! Guards! I order you to get them out of my sight! Now! Get them! Get them both!"

Farquaad was not going to let this little glitch stop him. He grabbed his crown from the podium and put it on. "All this hocus-pocus alters nothing," he announced. "This marriage is binding, and that makes me king!" He pointed to his crowned head. "See? See?" he said to everyone in general.

Following orders, the guards rushed in to grab Shrek and Fiona, separating them.

"No!" cried Shrek, struggling mightily.

"No, let go of me!" Fiona yelled. "Shrek!"

Shrek tried to fight his way toward her, but it was a losing battle. He was steadily being pulled away.

"Don't just stand there, you morons!" Farquaad shrieked at the guards. "Kill him if you have to—but get him!"

Still fighting, Shrek tried to break free of his captors.

"Insolent beast!" Farquaad screamed at him. "I'll make you regret the day we met. I'll see you drawn and quartered! You'll beg for death to save you."

"No! Shrek!" cried Fiona.

Farquaad now spun to face Fiona, who was being firmly held by the guards. He drew his sword and held it to her throat. "And as for you, my wife!" he snarled, "I'll have you locked back in that tower for the rest of your days!"

With a tremendous heave, Shrek managed to pull an arm free of the guards. Putting his fingers to his mouth, he emitted a piercing whistle.

"I am king!" yelled Farquaad. "I will have order! I will have perfection! I will have . . ."

Suddenly, the stained-glass windows behind the altar shattered, and in burst the dragon, with Donkey atop her head. Her fearsome mouth wide open, she swung down toward Farquaad.

"Arrrgggghhhhhhhhhh!" screamed Farquaad. But that was all he had time to say, because the dragon swallowed him up in one gulp. The crowd gasped in shock.

"All right!" hollered Donkey. "Nobody move! I got a dragon here, and I'm not afraid to use it!"

The terrified crowd froze.

"I'm a donkey on the edge!"

Suddenly, the dragon gave a great belch, and out shot Farquaad's crown.

"Celebrity marriages, they never last, do they?" quipped Donkey. The audience laughed and cheered. Then Donkey turned to the couple. "Go ahead, Shrek," he said.

Shrek stepped toward Fiona and gently put his hand on her shoulder, turning her toward him. She looked at him hopefully, expectantly.

"Um, Fiona . . . ?" said Shrek.

"Yes, Shrek?"

Shrek's eyes scanned Fiona's face. This time he was not going to chicken out.

"I love you," he said to her.

"Really?" she said.

"Really . . . really."

Fiona smiled. "I love you, too," she said.

Shrek broke into a matching smile. He leaned over and kissed her.

Getting into the moment, Thelonious grabbed

a sign from a nearby guard and scrawled "Ahhhhh" on it. He held up the sign. "Ahhhhh," sighed the crowd.

Fiona and Shrek finished their kiss, their eyes locked together. And then, all at once, Fiona began to lift into the air—and *glow*.

A strange, whispering wind began to whip up the air around them. And above the sound of the wind, an unearthly voice could be heard echoing through the church. "*Until you find true love's first kiss . . .*" the voice murmured.

Booom! The blinding flash of a magical explosion filled the cathedral, accompanied by a whirlwind of sparkling light that burst all the stained-glass windows at once. The light swirled through the room, twinkling as the sound of breaking glass tinkled all around them.

Then the magic subsided, and the voice began fading out, echoing down the vaulted spaces of the cathedral: "*. . . and then take love's true form . . . true form . . . true form . . .*"

Right beside Donkey and the dragon, one window happened to remain intact. It just happened to be a pane with the image of Lord Farquaad on it. They both looked at it for a moment—and then the dragon reached up and, with a flick of the claw, smashed the colored glass. They smiled.

Down on the floor of the cathedral, Fiona was now in a crumpled heap, her back to Shrek. He approached her gently. "Fiona? Are you all right?" he said, reaching down to help her up. She slowly turned around.

She was still an ogress.

Fiona looked down at herself, dismayed. "Well, yes . . . but, I don't understand," she muttered, mostly to herself. "I'm supposed to be beautiful."

"But you *are* beautiful," Shrek assured her.

Donkey couldn't take it anymore. "Aww," he sniffed sentimentally. "I was hoping this would be a happy ending."

And so it was. Anybody who saw Shrek kissing Fiona could tell.

nineteen
Into the Sunset

gre and ogress were joined in matrimony in Shrek's swamp. DuLocians and fairy-tale creatures celebrated side by side, with the dwarves providing the music. There was a fairy godmother present, and for the occasion she had turned the Three Blind Mice and an onion into a lovely carriage pulled by a team of white horses. The transformation hadn't been total, since the horses and driver were still blind and wearing dark glasses. But it looked pretty good.

Fiona and Shrek stepped into the carriage. But before she disappeared inside, Fiona turned and threw her bouquet into the assembled crowd. There was a brief melee as Sleeping Beauty and Snow White elbowed each other to catch it. But the dragon had the advantage of height, and intercepted it easily. She turned to Donkey, batting her long eyelashes and clutching the bouquet in her enormous jaws. Donkey just smiled back at her sheepishly.

Then it was time for the happy couple to leave. Shrek waved to Donkey from the back of the carriage as it began to move off.

At very the last moment, a tiny figure stepped out in front of the cheering crowd. It was the Gingerbread Man, on crutches but still gamely hobbling about. "God bless us, everyone," he cried.

And with that, Fiona and Shrek rode off into the sunset to begin their happily ever after.